I0631591

I   AIN'T   NO PROPHET

!!!

Short e-book version

WRITTEN BY

Eva Gaspar &

William A. Gaspar, MD

The Red Christmas 2021

RED CLOUD PROPHECY

ADAM & EVA Publishing

Holman, NM,

LEGAL DISCLAIMER

LIVING OR DEAD – ARE MADE UP
STORIES & COINCIDENTAL.

I

AIN'T

NO

PROPHET

!!!

Edited by

Rubin Xenia Gaspar

&

Austin Keane Gaspar

I Ain't No Prophet!

Published in the year 2021 in the United States.

ADAM & EVA Publishing

P.O. Box 241, Holman, N.M. 87723

Visit our website at www.adamevamedia.com

Or e-mail us at gaspar@redcloudprophecy.us

gasparvili@gmail.com

Library of Congress Cataloging-in-Publication D.

Gaspar, Eva 1954 –, Gaspar, Wm. A., 1957-

I ain't no prophet!!! Paperback version.

ISBN 978-1-7329085-4-3

Printed in the United States of America

Other books from these authors; **God's Generator, Sacred Cosmic Marriage, The**

1.

The Dream

"Are you a prophet Willy?" – the Voice asked. In my deep delta dream-state I was not sure who asked me. First, I could not open my eyes or turn my head. It felt like a real bad case of sleep paralysis. There were no actual sounds I heard, but my mind still absorbed the meaning. I could not muster up enough physical or mental energy to answer it. I wanted to say something, but no resonation was generated in my voice box. It felt like a year passed by. I heard myself gurgling. Finally, I thought, I pried my eyes open enough to notice a colorful light dancing on the ceiling. The illumination came through the open door of the bedroom and seemingly originated from the direction of our Christmas Tree. A dominant red streak caught my attention pointing to the fan above us. The Red Star from the top of the Christmas Tree was penetrating the darkness from the direction of the living room window on the East, just the same way I would notice the sunlight peak into the bedroom in the summer. Now I remembered. Last night was Christmas Eve. December 24ᵗʰ, 2020. 'What a year.' – I heard myself sighing in my dream.

I recalled that with a lot of care and preparation it was the crowning event of this holiday season that Eva and I were able to place that oversized illuminating red star wonder on top of the tree last night. We made a beautiful Christmas Tree that nobody will come to see because of the pandemic.

Being frustrated that I could not communicate with this mysterious voice, I robotically turned my head to the right as I followed the red illumination on the ceiling. I sheepishly looked over to my wife Eva, my eyebrows drawn demanding of her to assists me with an answer. She was unwillingly waking up next to me in my dream. Eva stared at me for a while and then was just smiling at my inability to respond. Strangely her hair was well done with just minimal tasteful make up on her face. Her smile was always bringing a reassuring happiness to my being, except today. I did not understand why she had her hair so well done in the middle of the night. The red illumination from the top of the tree was pointing to her forehead as if she was a Hindu Princess. The red dot now grew larger and appeared to be drilling down deep inside of her head, seemingly taking roots in her pineal gland. A pinecone emerged and sunk back into her head. It was surreal. Pineal gland, pinecone, pine tree for Christmas with a Red Star. Pretty strange. I did not realize that I must be dreaming and no need to be upset.

My concentration returned to Eva's situation. Her body slowly began to levitate out of the bed and the red dot on her forehead radiated intense heat that filled the room. A trickle of sweat ran down on my neck like it was a crawling bug. I smashed it to wipe it off.

"Are you a prophet Eva?" – the pleasant Male Voice now turned to my wife. It sounded like one of our ancient ancestors who already passed over and now tried to wake us up from a long dumb sleep. My grinning wife managed to sink back into the bed from her early morning levitation. None of us heard any sounds, but we both telepathically registered the repeated question. I enjoyed the fact that now the attention turned toward her. I stopped sweating and staired at my wife expecting her to produce a spiritually acceptable response. I hoped it would freeze that silly smile off her face before we get into trouble with the Male Voice. She kept grinning on - like she was possessed. I was hoping that she would stop giggling and produce a clever response, the sooner the better. Then it came.

"I ain't no prophet!!!" – finally we both shouted it out at the same time. It was insane synchronicity that we answered simultaneously as some freaky evil twins. We right away staired at each other and burst into an unstoppable laugh that sounded like drunk wild donkeys. Then suddenly the hysteria stopped. We did not know where it came from.

After a few painful moments staring at each other the miracle dissipated as fast as it began. Our responses surprised both of us. I never heard Eva use the improper double negatives. I, myself tried to avoid it as much as I could, except when it was cool. She always discouraged me to use improper English. An uneasy feeling developed in my belly that our life and happiness depended on finding the right answer to any questions this voice asked us.

'Was it the Voice of God talking to us?' – I wondered. I looked over to the other side of the bed again. My wife suspiciously appeared as a galactic goddess as she effortlessly got out of bed as an apparition. She still was sporting the red dot on her forehead, but the body now was radiating a golden yellow aura all around. 'I must be going crazy, … hmmm, too much eggnog last night?' – I was desperately trying to come up with an explanation to this out of body sensation. A magical presence of star dust was hanging in the air that began infusing into my being and now I was filled with joy and devoid of doubt. I knew who I was. I never remembered that my earthly body would feel this good. Not even when I did adrenochrome. Wait, I never did adrenochrome. That had to be another life.

"Come out to the living room honey, look who's here" – my beautiful fairy princess wife with the red dot was cooing me from the living room already.

With shinny flitter on her colorful dress my galactic goddess wife was summoning me from the direction of the radiating Christmas Tree. The red dot on her forehead now turned darker and had the appearance of venous blood pulsating out of a gunshot wound of a seared black hole.

Finally, I was able to look pass her and there he was. Santa Claus was standing there in full regalia by our Christmas Tree. Something was off, … something was not right about him. He looked like a radiant Tom Hanks. No beard and he was not overweight. 'What is this?' – I was asking myself. 'Santa went on the keto diet?' - I chuckled to myself. 'What did this world become? I got fatter and old fat Santa is shaving, getting into shape, may even does hot yoga?'

His red gown with the white fur gave him a hint of authenticity. Santa looked sharp and noble. Then from behind him emerged a round-faced smiling and well-fed brown-skinned dwarf. On further visual inspection he was clearly of African extraction. Round face, full lips, and strong brow ridge protected the eyes. He was a handsome young fellow. A strange purple, some would say indigo colored radiant aura surrounded his royal figure. There was an unseen strong ionizing electro-magnetic power emanating from this star child.

It was undeniably a physical pull that was hard to resist, one would want to give him a big fat hug.

"This is Bes, the original creator deity of Egypt" – Santa introduced his helper noticing my long stare.

"It is great to meet You, … your Honor" – I was awkwardly searching for the right title to use.

"Lord, I am your greatest fan" – Eva even out done me with the flattery. We knew that Bes was one of the most respected Creator gods of the ancient Egyptians. How important He was for humanity we did not yet grasp. He was the 'switcher of climate'.

"Santa, what is this unexpected visit about?" – I mustered up enough strength to express my curiosity. He pulled down on his red gown.

"You don't remember?!" – Santa staired at the both of us from right to left.

"Remember, … what" – Eva wondered.

Santa looked at Bes inquisitively. Bes shrugged his shoulders. Bes repositioned the trapeze shaped Red Crown on his head without losing the White Crown out of it. Santa looked back at us and asked.

"You two don't remember the prayers you muttered at the Christmas Tree last night while placing the Red Star on top?" – Santa turned and pointed to the top of the tree.

"Well, yeah … we wished and prayed to the Lord that we could promise each other that the next Christmas will be explosively much more fun and most memorable, … and we can spend it with our family." - I explained. Bes childishly clapped his hands together at my speech. Heat was released.

"It sure could be all of that on my repeat conception day." - Bes smiled knowingly at Santa.

"I prayed to our Lord that He would return in these biblical times and shake things up. I also summoned Moses, I trumpeted with our shofar, I called on the Native American Great Spirit, Crazy

Horse, the sleeping prophet Edgar Cayce, Napoleon Hill, the great horse of Attila, the Hun ... and all other spiritual beings, animal or human I could recall from beyond ... to interfere." – Eva rattled off a list of names, then gasped.

"... the horse of Attila?" – I asked unbelievably.

"I dreamt that ... the horse thing ... he was talking to me in my dream" – Eva tried to explain.

"In what language, in horse dialect?" – I laughed.

"Listen, you strange bed fellows." – Santa interrupted. He cupped his righthand fingers around his chin. "You both had powerful prayers. I could remind you more weird stuff, but it is enough to say that they were powerful verses that summoned us here." His stare caught Bes' eyes and they both sported secretive smiles.

"What do we supposed to do now? Recant, ... I mean, ... repent?" – Eva wondered.

"No, no, nooo! You both had some powerful wishes last night, and I would not be Santa Claus if I would not come here in a jiffy to answer your sincere prayers." – Santa smiled reassuringly. His mannerism would compete with any popular game show host. "We will have enormous fun."

"Ready to go?" – a radiant Bes turned to Santa.

"Are you already leaving?" – Eva asked.

12

"Yes, we are all leaving. All four of us are leaving for an exciting journey to find out if you are real prophets." – Santa smiled, leaned ahead, and looked at each of us separately. "Let us all go outside and pile into the sled." - Santa exclaimed jokingly.

We stepped outside the front door and snow was falling. The palm sized snowflakes looked like pink candy cane. It did not feel cold at all. Eva reached back behind the front door and grabbed her Michelangelo shawl to twirl around her neck. A golden chariot was parking at the curb with seven cinnamon colored rain deer prancing anxiously to fly away.

"Look, … Rudolph has the same red light shining on the tip of his nose that is swirling on Eva's head." – I proclaimed my discovery proudly.

"Good observation." – Santa shook his head approvingly. "Remember where you were shopping yesterday afternoon?" - He turned toward us.

"Macy's" – Eva answered quickly. "It was a going out of business sale … 60 % off everything!"

"Does Macy have a Red Star as a symbol?" – Santa cut in and asked with an honest stare.

"Yes, it does." – we agreed.

"What about the beer you drank last night?" – Claus looked at me with piercing eyes.

"I mostly drink Heineken." – I proclaimed.

"Does it have a red star on its label?" – Santa Claus continued with this kind of questioning.

"Yes, it does. … Coincidences?" – Eva offered.

"No coincidences! Especially, because you drank the S. Pellegrino mineral water. That is with a red star!" – Santa stated. "It is like the Star of Bethlehem on Christ's Birthday. All of these red stars are reminders of an ancient cosmic event that can soon become important." He looked up at us and paused to get the expected effect. We both looked lost. Santa finally had pity on us.

"This is the Milky Way in September. The red blazing Eastern Star comes from the forehead of the Galactic Virgin, where the Orion Nebula black hole is located. There is a reddish-brown dwarf star in the Trapezium constellation that is going through a birth cycle in that star nursery. It is allegorically the birth of Bes!" – Santa spoke with excitement. From the look of it, we appeared somewhat confused. The red star to us meant Christmas. And it meant the communist symbol on their flags - we did not like.

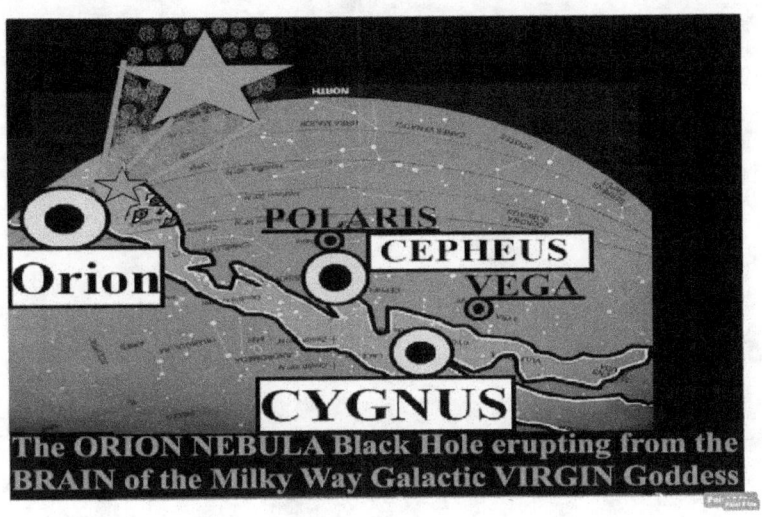

The ORION NEBULA Black Hole erupting from the BRAIN of the Milky Way Galactic VIRGIN Goddess

Santa Claus showed us the picture in the sky. The Galactic Virgin had the Red Blazing Star erupt from her Brain where the Orion Nebula black hole was.

"I show you another picture from the Gates of the Egyptian Book of the Dead." – Saint Nick was patiently explaining the Cosmic Mysteries.

"The last 12 – 14 years of 5,800 years long Climate Cycle is recorded down in every religion and creation mythology. **This is the Big Cosmic Secret!** It is hidden in the Egyptian Book of the

Dead, Christ's Last 12 hours on the Cross, Hercules 12 Labors, the 12 Knights of the Round Table. The last 12 Years of the Hero's Journey starts when he is 21 years old and ends when his is 33 years old." - He looked at us with searching eyes. His stare spiraled down into the depth of our souls. "As you may know there were two initial eruptions from the Orion Nebula black hole, which located in the Brain of the Milky Way Virgin. The first one was at Christmas as the allegorical conception of Jesus Christ. The second one of the series was in September of next year. That was the birth of the Cosmic Hero. Understand the Egyptian and Judeo-Christian teachings are about the natural cosmic events. Between the eyes of the Galactic Virgin of the Milky Way positioned the Orion Nebula black Hole. The 'cartouche' is the black hole eruption, the sacred pinecone from which the Christmas Tree grows out of the pineal gland of the Brain. The scientifically most important shape below is the Trapezium. **The TRAPEZIUM star constellation is where the Black Hole is positioned in the Orion Nebula. LOOK IT UP!"** - Santa looked possessed. – **"Bes, the Red Blazing Star eruption happens from the TRAPEZIUM star constellation."**

We looked mesmerized. The Brain part of the Milky Way – that Santa called the 'Galactic

Virgin' – certainly resonated with us on multiple levels, but we still needed clarifications on the Astronomy. Eva and I peered at each other and both of us understood that we became part of a group of cosmic secret keepers. The picture was amazing and revolutionary, but we did not know what to say. An uneasy quiet moment followed. We just stood there for about a minute. Finally, Claus broke the silence.

"Listen, we have been watching the two of you for a while. Willy, remember that your research started decades ago with a vision from the sky and a book. There came a few more books that you magically found for research." – Santa Claus explained.

"I remember. It was incredible! God and my dead Mom was talking to me." – I recalled.

"Step inside and bring me the book from your bookshelf titled '365 Starry Nights' from Chet Raymo." – Claus instructed me.

"Yeap, I remember, that was the third book that came to me in a strangely spiritual way." – I proudly stated as I went to fetch the book.

"Now, open it up on the January 13 – 14th page and read me this section." – he pointed to the page. Strangely, I had no question about reading well outside in the pitched dark night without lights.

"Here?" – I asked, pointing to the paragraph.

"Yes, read it out loud." - the old man agreed.

"13th: Embedded in the very heart of the Great <u>Orion Nebula</u>, and visible with binoculars or a small telescope, is the beautiful multiple star system known as the <u>Trapezium</u>, four hot young stars in a tight trapezoid-shaped cluster. Actually - these four stars are only the brighter components of an expanding cluster containing hundreds of faint stars. The intense radiation from these high-temperature stars excites the gas of the surrounding nebula and makes it glow. To the eye the nebula glows with an eerie green light, but photographs show beautiful hues of pink, blue and violet."

"See there!" – Santa excitedly interrupted. – "The blue, the green, the violet. ... This is what we will see at LORD Bes birth. We tried to get your attention to this scientific writing for decades. When you finally found the black hole references you showed interest again."

"The scientists from Cornell University did not reveal that there was a 'runaway black hole' in the Orion Nebula until 2012, and I sure did not know that it was in the Brain of the Milky Way Virgin." – I protested. - "I did not find the information until 2015, the Hebrew year of the Great Jubilee.

"Well, the Hebrew Year 5775 – is the beginning of the 7 years of Bounty. No wonder. … Listen, it is not your fault, … you even outlined the pages 20 years ago when it was not even known that we are dealing with the closest runaway black hole to Earth, … then your research stalled. … We had to try to get your attention from another direction. It was an act of God that we were finally able to get you back to these pages where you can discover the scientific facts about Bes' birth." – Santa explained. I nodded. "Read on! Read the next paragraph!" – Santa instructed me. First, I looked at the starry sky and falling stars were invading the darkness.

"14ᵗʰ: From the expansion rate of the <u>Trapezium</u> cluster and from the color and brightness characteristics of the member stars, it has been estimated that the stars in the group may be less than half a million years old – making it one of the youngest associations of stars known."

"I have to interrupt here." – Santa Claus cut in.

We looked up to see what clarifications He will suggests on the quote. "The star cluster is closer to 1 million years old. That is when the 116,000 years old Milankovitch Ice Age rhythm began." – He stated with confidence.

"What was it before?" – I asked with genuine interest.

"It was the 41,000 years rhythm. … So, human heartbeat in its current form is 1 million years old. A new human heartbeat was born a million years ago." – the old Man of Winter stated with confidence. It was a little surprising to us.

"So, the magical Orion Nebula star nursery is only then 1 million years old?" – Eva chimed in with curiosity.

"No, the new developing stars of the Trapezium star cluster is only 1 million years old with the 116,000 years long heartbeat of a full Ice age. The whole Orion Nebula is about 3.3 million years old. That is when the 41,000 years old rhythm began." – Santa Claus stated. – "Nobody considers that as a natural power source in human evolution."

"Wait, wait …!" – Eva got suddenly excited. Santa turned toward her with an expressive face of wonder. – "Then what if the Orion Nebula 'BRAIN' is what allows humans to live on Earth and be smart? – She sounded logical. Santa nodded.

"You're 100 % right!" – Saint Nick replied. "Good observation Eva. Willy, continue with the quote." – Santa looked at me.

I started back reading the rest of the quote on Bes.

"Indeed, some members of the group may even now be "turning on" their nuclear energy sources to become stars. As gravity pulls together a knot of gas and dust from the Great Nebula, the pressure at the core of the contracting cloud goes up. When the temperature reaches about 10 million degrees Celsius, nuclei of hydrogen atoms fuse together to form the heavier nuclei of helium. This is the same process that occurs in the explosion of a hydrogen bomb and result in a release of energy. The energy makes its way to the surface of the contracting sphere where it is radiated as heat and light. A star is born!" – I looked up. Santa was animated mimicking an explosion from his brain and at this point reminded me of a half insane Dr. Brown from the movie 'Back to the Future".

"A star is born!" – Santa echoed the last sentence. "Bes is born from the Orion Furnace black hole. This is the reason for the Christmas celebration. ...

This book was written in 1981. The same year you had your first vision, the same year you came to the US and the same year your mother died at an early age. Does it start making sense? So, someone real close to you channeled this one to you on our advice." – Claus smiled lovingly. At this point I did not know how to respond.

"It was a little early on your journey, but we had to get it to your attention. It took you a few years, … decades even, to get it." – Santa Claus informed me as he stood up tall. We could not see anything, no sky, no stars, just an enormous Santa Claus.

"You have been watching me, … us, for decades?" – I turned my head toward my wife to see her reaction while scratching my head nervously. I was more than surprised, I was stunned. I started gesturing with my hands to say something, but nothing worthy came to my mind. So, it was Santa Claus & Co., who was watching me, not the NSA.

"Yes, on the insistence of your mother and the Spiritual Committee on Re-Creation." – Santa calmly explained. "She thought that you both could stand the scrutiny of Truth. She gave up a lot to send you this message. So, don't be upset."

"So, why she - who really did not believe in religious ideas … joined You - Santa, and maybe others … and the two of You wanted me to know about the fact that there was a star nursery in the Orion Nebula?" – I squeezed my temples of my head with my palms hard to get my mind clearer.

"This is not about blind faith in any religion, but it is about the knowledge of the Cosmic RE-CREATION of the ages!" – Santa Claus emphasized. "God's Natural Law." – He claimed.

"What?" – I asked with confusion in my voice.

"I am talking about the 'true cosmic religion' that explains the science!" – Santa insisted.

"Explain it then, please!" – I calmed down a little.

"Okay, you grew up in a neighborhood with Jewish, Catholic, communist and agnostic people." Santa started out. – "Did they all believe in the same Universal God?" I shook my head in disagreement. "Okay, let us start with the Catholic Faith. Remember, the Creation of Adam painting by Michelangelo in the Vatican? We both nodded.

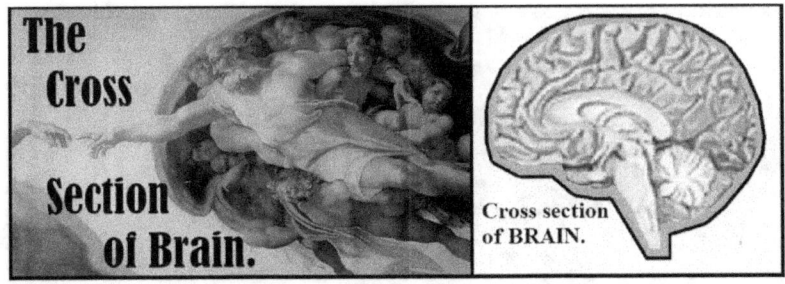

The
Cross

Section
of Brain.

Cross section
of BRAIN.

"The mauve background behind God is the cross section of a Brain. The Brain of the Galactic Virgin, which houses the Orion Nebula! On that painting the Trapezium star constellation falls to where the Heart of God is. That is not religion, it is science!" – He boiled with passion. "Red Blazing Star that appears from the brain in the eruption of the Orion Nebula. The red star symbol is present with the Catholics, the Jews, the Communists and the Agnostics." – Santa Claus informed us further.

"So, none of these stories are about pharaohs and princesses? All of these tales are hiding the cosmic secrets?" - I asked with surprise.

"Cosmic science - what is hidden in these stories. This black hole eruption from the Trapezium star constellation can happen again in 2021 - 2022." – Santa Claus confidently stated as he flashed a picture in front of us. "That is the Egyptian Last Supper. It is also part of Christ teaching. The message is that after the eruption of the Orion Nebula black hole from the brain of the Milky Way Virgin – in September 2022 in the Virgo sign – you will eat your last great meal. Early harvest, then the Seven Years of Famine will intensify in 2022."

"Wow, how did I miss that?" – I asked.

"The Red Blazing Star coming from the Brain of the Galactic Virgin is not obvious here. Now, that we are looking at it with the knowledge of Astronomy and Cosmology in the Egyptian Mysteries, it is much more obvious, isn't it?" – the Old Man of Winter looked at us with vindication. "You could have not known this in the 1980's, 1990's or even up to 2012." – Santa explained. "Initially, you just began to learn English when you came across this book and at the same time both of you started to go to college. … And most importantly, the scientists did not tell anybody that there was a runaway black hole in the star nursery of the Orion Nebula until 2012." – Santa informed us. "Now we know the eruption comes from the Orion Nebula's Trapezium star constellation."

"I could not connect these parts. It seems little more obvious now." – I offered. I felt less guilty not finding the answers earlier.

"We really had a hard time trying to build a celestially driven case to get your attention about the Secret of Bes coming out of the Orion Nebula black hole that was located in the Brain of the Galactic Virgin." – the old man explained.

"I do not even remember, how we got to the Orion Nebula in the Brain of the Virgin from the Ice Age cycles?" – I wondered.

"Initially, the first book about the Ice Age cycles brought your attention to the heartbeat of Earth. The second book we channeled to you was a work from Dr. David Ulansey on the astronomy of The Origin of the Mithraic Mysteries, remember. That is when you called the professor in California. He gave you the name of a few writers. He told you to talk to John Major Jenkins, the author of the Maya Cosmogenesis 2012. Then you became friends with John, and you were pulled into the Mayan Calendar. … It took us three decades to bring you up to speed. You needed to go to medical school first then become a Native American Indian, raised and initiated, then to go the Vatican Museum and Egypt. There was some big resistance until 2015 – 2016 until we passed the Great Jubilee. A number of times we succeeded getting through Eva who pulled you into some of the related mysteries." – Santa explained. "You were totally lost at times for years! I am glad you are both back."

"You were channeling us information all those years?" – I asked. I was not surprised as I felt it and Eva did too, at times. We just did not know who was sending us information from the Ether.

Angels, spirits, Jesus, Moses, God, relatives? – we did not understand, but now it starts making sense.

"Everybody gets angelic messages?" – Eva asked with curiosity.

"Yes, but naturally not everybody listens, … and after a while we stop trying." – the old man explained. He had both of his palms cuffed around his ears. "They usually find a hobby, sport, start drinking, doing drugs, so they don't have to listen." Santa said with conviction. "That's the majority."

"Well, … It makes sense now. Initially, … I felt that I was going crazy. So, I stopped listening, … I wanted to feel normal" – I admitted. - "Now, knowing about the Black Hole in the Trapezium of Orion Nebula clears things up.". – I confessed.

"We were successful to make you study the Egyptian mysteries, the Mayan creation legends, the cosmic subjects, religion, astronomy, Babylonian creation mythology, Jewish mysticism, Cosmology, languages, art, … but we had a difficult time to make the logical and meaningful scientific connections between the subjects we channeled the two of you." - Santa informed.

"That explains to me the unrelenting, unexplainable and insane spiritual push I felt since 1981 to study these seemingly unrelated subjects.

Okay, I am not crazy." – I sighed in relief. I looked at Eva who nodded in agreement. We both seemed to have some tears generating in our tear ducts. I felt confused and emotional. I was not sure what interest the other side had in convincing me of anything. I studied Eva's face to see what was she thinking? – I almost cried, but something held it back. She offered her take on it.

"I did not want to read as much, but I enjoyed experiencing things, praying, meditating, observing different cultures, visiting churches, synagogues, basilicas, getting involved in ceremonies … like the Native American sweat lodge and Sundance. That is how I learn, … by doing it." – Eva happily exclaimed. – "I am a people's person." – she added.

"It is all good! The mysteries will all be tied together." – the old man smiled mysteriously. Eva clapped in joy like a crazed cheerleader.

"Before we leave on an exciting celestial journey" – he extended both of his arms toward us and then pointed to the sky with them. We all looked up. "We need to start naming and recognizing things astronomically to have a clear understanding of what symbolizes what." – He smiled. - "We shall learn the cosmic secrets."

"We shall learn the cosmic secrets?" – I mumbled.

"From here on, there are no men, no women, no human gods, no humans, no history. Read the stars." – He looked up. – "We are only concerned with God's Amazing Cosmos. The key is Astronomy."

"We are going to celebrate the red blazing star, the 'birth of Bes' at next Christmas?" – Eva was leaning down, smiling and had her arm comfortably around the shoulders of Bes. "Should it be Jesus, rather?" – Eva asked. The Red Hyena watched her intently.

"Bes is the reason for the season!" – Santa jovially explained. "It starts next Christmas 2021 and 2022!"

"I thought that same exact wisdom – 'reason and season' - was said about Jesus?" – I muttered.

"Every religion celebrates Bes scientifically, whether it is Egyptian, Sumerian, Hindu, Judaism or Christianity. The Birth and periodic Re-Birth of Bes, the Brown Dwarf star in the Orion Nebula at the Trapezium star constellation every about 5,800 years is the event that every culture, every prophet allegorically teaches us to celebrate. That is the cosmic religious unity. That knowledge is what holds together humans. This is wisdom. Bes' birth is the only scientific one. Every other sacred teaching is just an important reminder of the celestial event." – Santa was convinced about this.

"Every culture?" – I wondered.

"Yes. Every culture, no exceptions. It was some of your ancestors, the members of the Sumerian Magyar tribe along with the Hebrews who went down to Egypt over 5,000 years ago to re-record the celestial story in the Valley of the Kings. That is why linguistically the two of you are ahead of other students to learn these enigmas faster, because some of the important words of Astronomy and Cosmology are familiar to you in your own languages. Did you notice?" – Santa enquired.

"Which words do you mean?" – Eva asked.

"There are a lot of important words you will find in these creation mythology stories that are straight out of your ancient Magyar language. The word to 'measure', the word for 'bee', 'iron rod' and others can help you recognize what the cosmic story is about." – Santa stated with confidence.

"So, all of these stories are about a cosmic event that was started with an eruption from the Orion Nebula black hole, which started the climate change." – I summarized my thoughts.

"Yes, it is all about the Egyptian creation god Bes. Let us learn about him. Okay, here is a picture of Bes the ancient Egyptian deity of the Orion Nebula black hole's star nursery" – Santa pulled up a picture. "Does not our Bes look just like him?" – Santa Claus smiled proudly.

"Jesus Christ, Krishna, Mitra and even the Scorpion King came down at Christmas to teach this very important cosmic fact." – Santa claimed. "That is why they all celebrate their birthdays on the same day of the year." – It was a strange statement from Santa Claus. - 'If Santa does not know what happens at Christmas, then who does?', - I was thinking to myself. A totally different door opened to us.

"So, how come that we have never even heard about this cute little cosmic Ruddy Brown Dwarf?" – Eva was genuinely curious.

"I am from above, … celestial. I represent the Cosmic Mysteries. Humans think about human history. They named their different gods as human heroes in memory of Bes for thousands of years. Initially it was obvious that they all celebrated what happened 5786 years ago, and when they all forget the original cosmic holiday, they all learned a different language and then they went out to kill each other in ugly wars, … in the name of their human gods. If everybody would have kept the original Cosmic Bes birthday and the knowledge of the ONE Universal GOD, then there would be no wars over religions. Everybody wants to own God, but nobody wants to understand the scientific reasons." – Santa had a hint of sadness in his voice.

"So, because humans do not want to understand God's Natural Law … that allows the religious and spiritual leaders to come up with moral human stories, install their righteous or twisted control … claiming that they received their mandate from God … that maybe just made up, … but underneath they can still teach us the hidden cosmic events? They could not just tell us what is going on in Nature, how things are arranged by God's design? Why cannot our leaders be honest?" – Eva wondered.

"I tell you from experience. We have not been able to find humans in large numbers who could absorb and tolerate the Truth that is emanating from God. Most humans over the generations are the enemies of scientific knowledge. Humans always change God to their local deities, animal gods, or human gods that they can then form into their desired mold. Humans are not satisfied with the real God, so they make up their own. Since, they have their own slice of pizza, now they can war over it." – Santa Claus explained. "Bes is the biggest Scientific Secret of the recurrent Sacred Cosmic births and re-births of planets and stars! You know that our Perfect God, the Shepherd King is the only Scientist in this whole big Universe and everything we will teach you shall celebrate that! You can think of Bes as a Cosmic

Son of God. It is science, the story cannot be corrupted." – Santa whispered. "Cosmic events are recorded down in symbolic religious arts and ceremonies." - He became animated and energized. "Bes symbolizes the Cosmic Birth. This is what the Son of God, Christ's conception at Christmas, birth in September and re-birth at Easter teaches us allegorically." – Santa smiled reassuringly. "The birth of Bes is the birth of the Christ, the recurrent cosmic secret that switches the climate from hot to cold and back. Bes and the swan black holes are the secret switches of the climate every 5,786 years." – Santa exclaimed. We nodded and he continued.

"Now, if something can tilt the climate from hot to cold every roughly 5,800 years as clockwork, it has to be a very important secret." – Santa continued with the important science he needed to teach us.

"Why is he called the 'secret', ... I mean why Bes is the secret?" – I asked.

"The actual ancient Egyptian word 'BES' means "SECRET". They both spelled and pronounced the same. Bes is the Secret because his name straight means and spells 'secret' in hieroglyphic Egyptian. Brilliant!" – Santa became animated again.

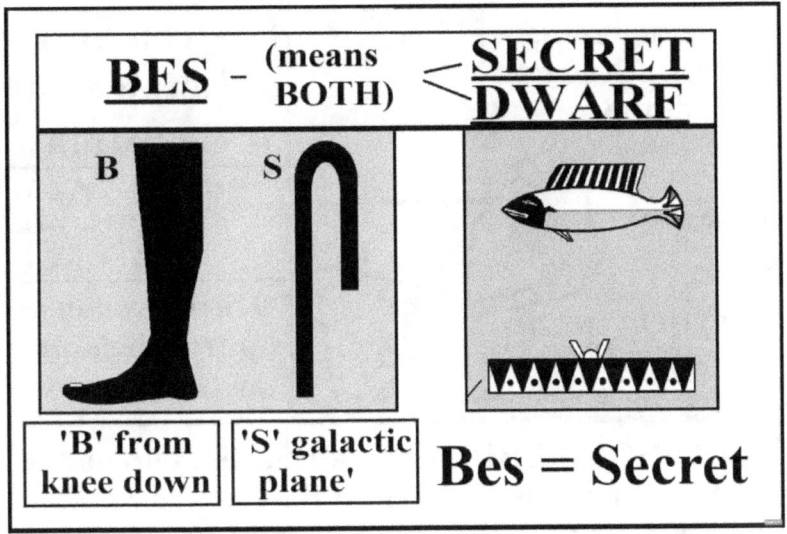

"How does Bes switch the Ice Age cycles so exactly?" – Eva wondered. "Why at Christmas?

"God releases his 'VOICE', and it comes on time. That vocal RADIATION activates our Galaxy. In the Milky Way Orion lines up on the plain of the Orion Cygnus Arm at Christmas in the East direction when it erupts." – the Old Man stated. – "Here is a picture. Christ tried to teach the same."

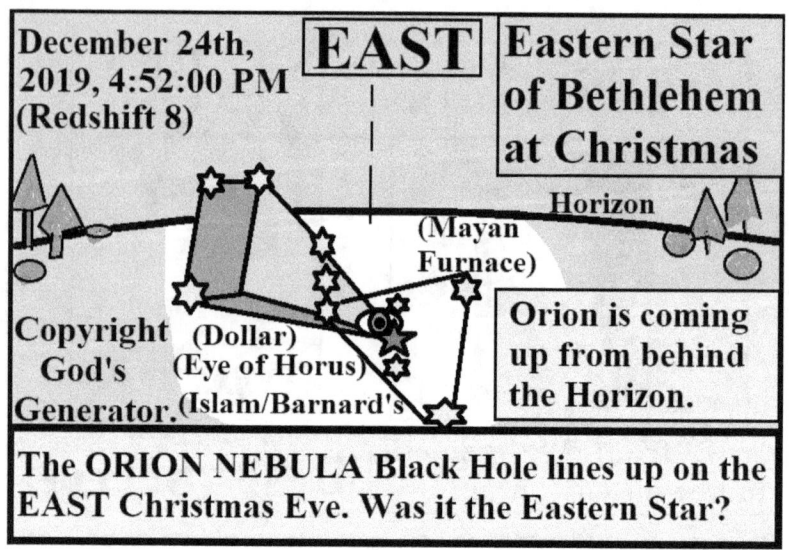

The following text appears within the image boxes:

December 24th, 2019, 4:52:00 PM (Redshift 8)

EAST

Eastern Star of Bethlehem at Christmas

Horizon

(Mayan Furnace)

Copyright God's Generator.

(Dollar)
(Eye of Horus)
(Islam/Barnard's

Orion is coming up from behind the Horizon.

The ORION NEBULA Black Hole lines up on the EAST Christmas Eve. Was it the Eastern Star?

"Well, the Orion Nebula black hole EYE is lined up in the East on Christmas Eve. We have been talking about Bes and the Orion Nebula black hole all this time, but then the STAR OF BETHLEHEM is the same event, right." – Santa pulled up another picture on his cosmic I pod. - "This should worth a dollar." – Santa Claus grinned at us mysteriously.

"It's worth much more than a dollar!" – I blurted it out in a pious excitement. Eva looked at me.

"It is worth ONE DOLLAR!" – she emphasized with faked anger directed at me as she smiled. I felt confused, not understanding why she argues with me. I was stunned and could not answer back right away. I must've looked dumb. Eva took pity on me.

"The upper part of Orion makes an upside-down pyramid whose top points to the EYE of the Orion Nebula. That is apparently one of the secrets of the ONE DOLLAR BILL!" – her voice screeching with excitement, as if she was a Swooping Hawk going after a pray. She must have just realized the awesome wisdom Saint Nicholas was teaching us.

"Wow, that is amazing. The ONE DOLLAR BILL was designed to commemorate the BIRTH OF BES, ... and our Lord Jesus Christ ...?" – I was excited.

"... and Krishna, and Mitra, and the Scorpion King!" – my wife completed my sentence. "... but then who are You – Santa Claus – in this cosmic mystery?" – Eva curiously probed the Old Man.

"I am both Perseus and Orion, and the driver of the chariot pulled by the Taurus Bull aka Reindeers. The Cosmic Mysteries that we teach is simple and constructed out of exact Astronomy." – Santa remarked as he turned to me. "Start with Orion."

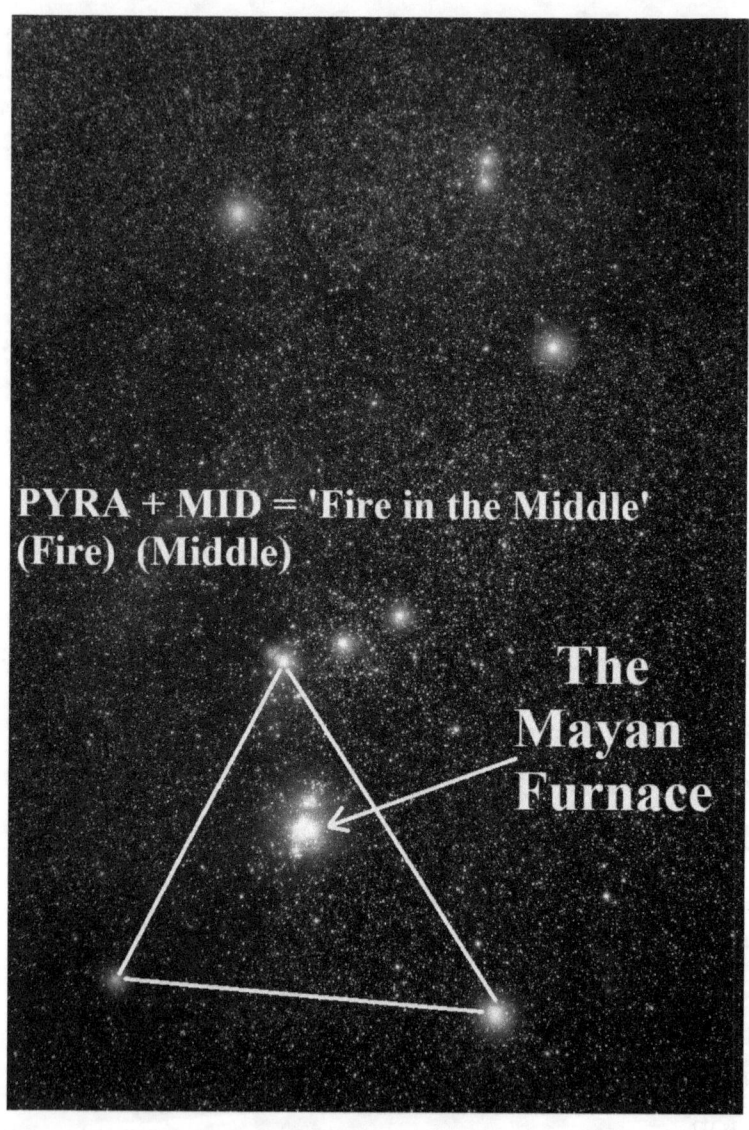

"Here is Orion. The Mayans told you where the FURNACE is, right?" – Santa said. "Connect the other stars above to get the upside-down pyramid."

We were surprised that we could see that. Before we could ask a question, Santa pulled up another picture of Orion from the sky with markings.

"Okay, look at this now." – the old man said.

Barnard's Loop

"Here the same upside-down pyramid is present, but now we can see the symbol of Islam hidden in the Barnard's Loop CRESCENT!" – Santa stated.

"That is amazing!" – Eva shouted in celestial joy.

"I understand the upside-down pyramid pointing down to the Orion Nebula black hole EYE, I also see that the Mayan's marked the FURNACE of the SKY in the same black hole position, … but what is the Barnard's Loop, I never heard of it?" – I asked.

"Since there is a black hole in the Orion Nebula at the Trapezium star constellation, it puts out IONIZING RADIATION in a circular fashion. As we observe it from Earth, it only looks like a CRESCENT shape from this angle. That was the ancient symbol on coins - almost all cultures used 2 – 3,000 years ago from Babylonia, Israel, Sumer, the Byzantine Empire that is now Turkey, the Greeks, Romans, and everybody else. At least now you know that it is NOT the Moon that the Crescent represents, but it is the Ionized Field of the Black Hole. Now, with this ancient mysterious Crescent we are back to BES, the famous reddish BROWN DWARF star of the Orion Nebula black hole." – Santa Claus proudly exclaimed.

"It almost starts looking like all ancient religious symbols somehow hide the star knowledge of the Orion Nebula black hole 'furnace' and the Cygnus Swan / Northern Cross secrets." – I concluded.

"We could count how many religions display the same cosmic phenomenon." – Cutie chimed in.

"Willy, you still have Chet Raymo's book with you?" – Santa asked patiently. I nodded. "Open it up on the first page that marks the January 1st date, just a few days passed Christmas. Show us the picture of the Milky Way sky on that day." – Santa Claus instructed me. It looks toward the South. I opened the page and showed it to him. It looked a little different. It was hiding Santa and the chariot.

"Think of the TWO BROTHERS of creation mythology from all over the world. From right to left, PERSEUS, Bull Reindeer with Pleiades, Orion by the Milky Way River, the Chariot, and the Dog, Sirius." – Santa pointed out. – "Thus, the sacred history of Re-Creation of the ice age cycles is recorded in the stars." – Saint Nick exclaimed.

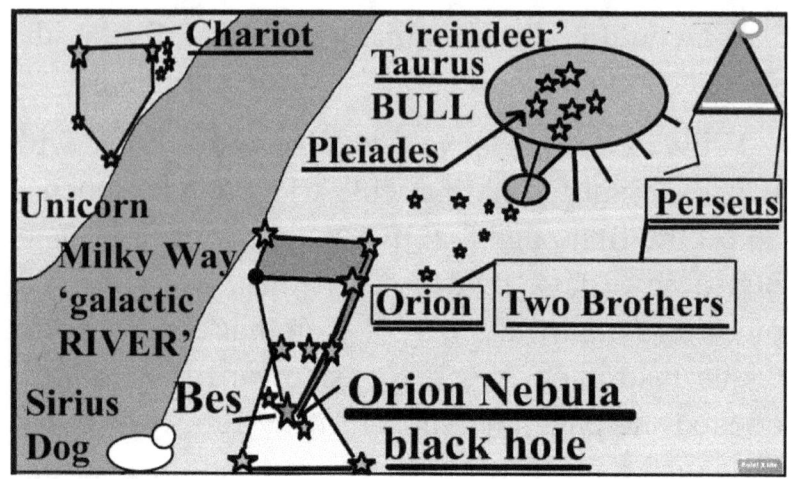

"Your teachers never taught you to look at space and see what star constellations are in the sky in the four directions at the holidays." - Saint Nick stated. He rubbed his nose intensely until it turned red. "As Santa Claus, I came mainly as Perseus, the First Brother in mid-December. I like to think of myself as a composite of a number of concepts, I also represent the FATHER, ORION and PERSEUS." – Santa proclaimed. He pulled his chest out. "I am Nimrod the Great Hunter, and I am also his two sons." – He laughed whole-heartedly. I felt confused. "I am the beginning and the end."

"What part is Perseus in you Santa?" – my wife interrogated the old man with an acquired rigor.

"My pointy hat is from Perseus, the first brother of the two brothers of creation mythology." – Santa answered and added. "Perseus started the early events in December".

"What about Orion …?" – Eva persisted.

"My Red and White regalia is the Unification hidden in the Orion black hole and the geo-dynamo. The 'illumination' at Christmas comes from Orion." – the old man educated us. "The World Tree, the eruptions, the Shaman travelling as Santa Claus in the sky. I was teaching this to the Euro-Asiatic and Native American tribes, … what happened to that knowledge? Disappeared?" – Santa paused

"The Euro-Asiatic ancient shamans depicted me on their sacred drums several thousands of years ago. This was before Judaism or Christianity existed. But I existed and my cosmic teaching existed. The people with today's modern religions and re-makes - think that they invented me or worse yet, that they own me. Time made us all to forget the ancient sacred scientific knowledge." – Santa Claus concluded.

2.

The Two Brothers.

We were hanging out with Santa in front of the house occasionally looking up at the sky and enjoying the high-quality mythological discussion he gifted us with. There was no barking of dogs in the neighborhood, and I don't remember the sounds of passing cars. We knew that there was so much more we needed to learn, but at this point we could not think of anybody else who would lay it out so clearly for us. Bes and the animals were sleeping on the chariot, and we did not feel tired, we were not thirsty or hungry and most importantly we did not have to go to the bathroom. Everything being sad felt like it took only 68 seconds and not any longer, although the real human time had to be close to an hour. The temperature outside was perfect. We were waiting for Santa Claus to plan the next step.

"We would like to learn and understand the Two Brothers of Creation Mythology and how they define the seasons and actions that are attributed to them. I understand that it has to be more exact than how our old understanding dictated it." – Eva was asking the Old Man of Winter for clarifications.

"Here is a picture to show you Perseus and Orion the TWO BROTHERS. First, we saw them on December 25th. This picture I am showing you two are the Two Brothers coming together as the Two Axes of the Earth. They came together in an axis shift union on March 26 about 4 years after the December conception and the September birth.

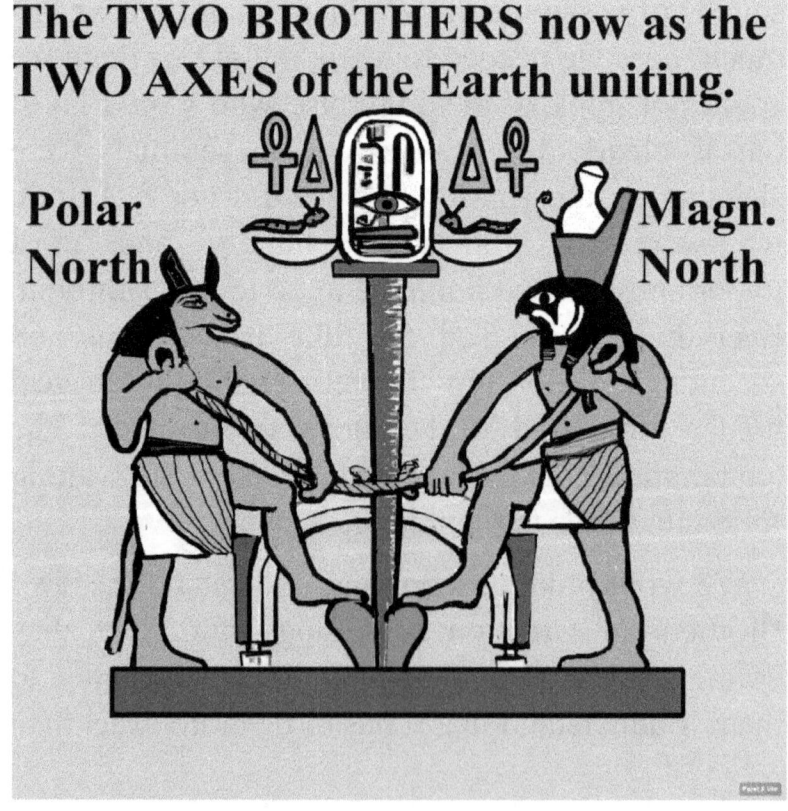

The TWO BROTHERS now as the TWO AXES of the Earth uniting.

Polar North

Magn. North

"The TWO BROTHERS who begin at Christmas at Bes cosmic conception, continue to the cosmic birth in next September, and will unite in the HEART OF THE BULL, which is the PLEIADES star constellation 3 and a half years later. This journey takes 3 ½ to 4 years as we learned the time of the biblical anti-Christ. At the end of the 3 ½ years Horus and Set, as the Magnetic North and the Polar North unite. They will be killing the Bull, the Golden Elk, or the Golden Calf on MARCH 26. roughly 4 years later after the initial Christmas. That is the 4th 'Hour' or the 4th Year of that journey that started the climate changes. The Magyar Egyptian Sumerians called the Northern Cross CYGNUS by the name of NÉGY ('nedj'), which in their language means 'FOUR'. Now, one could think that is a coincidence being the FOURTH year, but on this holiday of Passover the Jewish children need to ask 4 questions, the adults need to drink 4 glasses of red wine or grape juice. They need to recline. Touch the head to the knee."
– It was hard to follow the great Saint Nick. "On top of that, at this ancient holiday the Native Americans, the Apache tribe celebrate the Dark Demon who rises in 4 steps at the Pleiades. The southwestern Indian tribes celebrate it with the

Lizard symbol. The lizard looks like 4 steps when looked at on March 26 Eastern toward the East. Lot of star constellations to learn!" – Santa concluded.

"The two brothers appear three times around the year. You have to remember these distinctions, but also remember that the two different brothers become the same concept on March 26th. THEY UNITE!" – Claus looked up to see agreeing faces, but we were somewhat lost. "These two brothers, Perseus and Orion with the Bull in between them appear 3 times in December, end of March, and September. So, the stories involve all the religious holidays. That makes it difficult to identify the season when always the same two brothers and the bull or calf play their part." – Santa explained.

It seemed that we need a lot of repetitions before we digest these two brothers of different mothers. I began to wonder who organized the world-wide creation stories to such an accuracy that it would match on every continent. Even more so, 'could it be a little simpler, please' – I was thinking it to myself.

"Orion and Mitra are the Bull killing brothers, just as Gilgamesh and Enkidu are the two brothers in the Epic of Gilgamesh who kill Humbaba the powerful celestial Bull. Now, in Egypt when they show the 'two drilling brothers' who drill into

Mother Earth, those two brothers are Horus and Set on the above picture. They drill into the Heart of the Elk or Bull, which is the Pleiades. Then you have the biblical brothers Abel and Cain and after that Seth."

"Even the biblical two brothers are like Perseus and Orion?" – I asked.

"Yes. There is no difference between religion or mythology. It is all about Astronomy." – Santa claimed with a straight face. "Now, those two brothers also represent the two axes of the Earth's geo-dynamo, the Magnetic North and the Polar North." – Santa exclaimed.

"That is the difficult part, Santa. Are they two brothers, two stars constellations or the TWO AXES of the Earth?" – I asked to show my confusion. "It sounds more complicated than one would expect." – I admitted.

"The Two Brothers are all of that, but most importantly the Two Axes of the geo-dynamo come out of our Earth. That is the case with the biblical Boaz and Jachin, who again represent the Magnetic North and the Polar North pillars. A little bit confusing. It will be repeated. You will learn from different disciplines of the S.A.L.S.A. - Seven Ancient Liberal Sacred Arts." – Santa smiled.

"I am a visual learner. I hope, they will show us pictures?" – I was hopeful.

"They will show you pictures. You will need to brush up on the Astronomy of different seasons and different directions of that holiday season." Santa stated.

"Learn the astronomy of the religious holidays in every season, first?" – I asked.

"Yes. Start with the first cosmic holiday. The Two Brothers and the EASTERN sky at Christmas, do you remember which animal star constellations were present on December 24th on the EAST, next to the Sun on the Roman founding brothers' birth?" – Nick asked. He made an angry canine face.

I must have displayed a confused look on my face.

"I am talking about ROMULUS and REMUS who founded Rome on the Seven Hills." – the old man stated. He looked up with a big smile.

"I remember those two, but I cannot recall the related star constellations." – I pleaded as a guilty senator. My face was distorted into false thinking.

"The WOLF!" – Santa sang it with high pitch.

"That is right, the Lupus WOLF mother who is feeding Romulus and Remus. It is all over in the Vatican." – my wife was shouting it out with joy.

"Look on this picture in Egypt around December. In the eastern direction, we can see the Frog early December representing Perseus and water, then at Christmas time is the Wolf. Lupus Wolf is the mother of Romulus and Remus, the Two Founding Brothers of Rome. It is pure Astronomy. Here it is the year 2022." – Santa explained the picture.

"So, this picture represents the beginning of the climate changes 5786 years ago in early December, ... that is parallel to 2021 or 2022?" – Eva asked politely. "The wolf is always at Christmas?"

"Yes. It could be 2021, but it is most likely 2022. In mythology Perseus is born on the raging sea. That happens after the September tsunami. The cosmic boat begins a few weeks later right after the Wolf. Here we don't see it, but the Scorpion is right above the Wolf in the eastern sky on December 25th. The fact that we see the Vulture right above the beginning of the boat, also carries a warning for the future." – Saint Nick was patiently explaining. He held up his palms connected by the thumbs to mimic a bird with outstretched wings. "Earthquake, Polar North – Anubis Wolf shaken from its Core!"

"So, what I am hearing here is that since it is Christmas, it represents Jesus Christ, … but then the Lupus Wolf is mother to Romulus and Remus before Christ, and even before that time, this December is also the place of the Scorpion King of Egypt? All the same events?" – my wife asked as she was circling her index finger in front of her.

"Yes! You seem to start understanding that every culture astronomically talks about the same time-period. You might even become a prophet." – Santa winked his left eye at her encouragingly. Eva bowed with arms outstretched to resemble a fairy angel.

"I will need to learn much more." – Eva politely answered back. "Astronomy is a vast subject."

"The Scorpion at Christmas! ... Have you two heard about the first Egyptian King, the SCORPION KING being the parallel hero of Jesus Christ?" – Santa was lightly chuckling as he asked. "As matter of fact, I heard that Dwayne Johnson, the Rock is thinking about remaking the Scorpion King movie this year. That would be very timely and appropriate."

"He is buff, but he is getting up in age." – Eva commented. – "There were a lot of running, jumping and escaping from those two serpents." She stated. "Then the two serpents represent two early black hole eruptions." – Eva concluded.

"The Astronomy of the Scorpion came to Egypt from the Sumerian Magyars. About 5,000 years ago the Royal Harp was made and then buried in the King's Grave in southern Iraq. That is where your ancestry originates from. I am talking about the Magyar tribe." – Santa sounded mysterious. "So, time on the Harp starts with the bottom picture. It is 2021 and 2022 today." - Santa Claus looked up at us. "Looking at the Royal Harp, the Scorpion is the beginning of the end on this picture in Sumer, also. We have dispersed the Natural Cosmic Truth on every continent. So, let me show you the BULL-HEADED LYRE OF UR of the Sumerians. This is one of the oldest stringed instruments, the scientists dug up. It is now housed and being restored in the Penn Museum in Philadelphia." – Santa explained.

"Why did they enclose the knowledge in a Harp?" – my wife wondered.

"Very good!" – the old man was shaking his head approvingly. "The HARP and the HAWK defines the direction of the MAGNETIC NORTH. It was unearthed in the mid-1800's from the Royal Tomb of the famous Babylonian King. Most of the biblical stories began in Babylonia. So, the VEGA star – that represents the Magnetic North – is the main star of the Lyre Harp star constellation. So, the Vega HAWK star and the HARP star constellation is very important!" – Santa Claus emphasized.

He seemed happy that he could connect the harp to the Magnetic North of the geo-dynamo of the Earth. It started to become increasingly clear that Santa Claus was all about teaching us Astronomy and Cosmology with special emphasis on how the direction of the stars connected to the function of the Earth and how it is hidden in the mythology.

"So, from bottom to top, these are the first four years of the Last 14 years. It is biblical before the Bible, or the Torah was constructed on this ancient information. Christmas in Egypt and Sumer is marked by the Scorpion, the September eruption of

Orion is commemorated with the Mountain GOAT as we will see and the marker for the ORION NEBULA is the 'Kanna' can vase (Khnemu)." – Santa explained. It was too much to take in.

"Do we have the two brothers and the bull again in the fourth year?" – I asked.

"The lyre itself is 'bull-headed'. That connects you to the Taurus Bull and the Pleiades. Here the Sumerians did it a little more comically. The two brothers here are two bulls and the bull itself is a human. Confusing." – Santa explained.

"I am so glad that you are here Santa and try to walk us through the Astronomy, tying the cosmic events to the pictures. We would never been able to solve this ourselves." – I claimed.

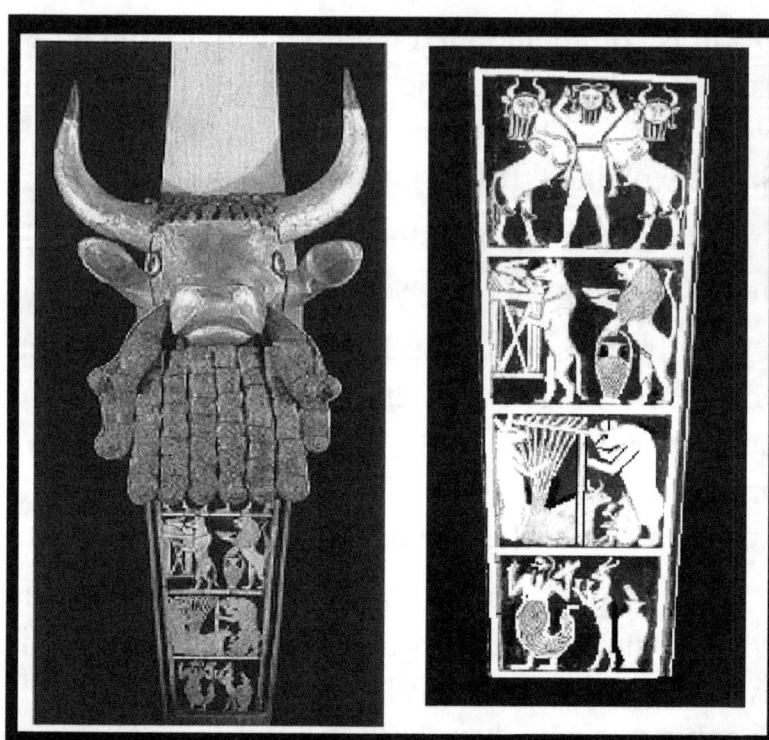

Sumer Babylon HARP.
Time starts bottom up.
SCORPIO, GOAT and
the Secret 'can' Kanna.

"The SCORPION here represents the time of Christmas on the East, today parallel date would be December 25th, 2021- 2022"- Santa looked up.

"The Mountain Goat is Capricorn, who one would expect to see beginning in late December, but as we remember – it shows up a few months earlier on the NORTHERN SKY. As matter of fact, it is in the sky around the FALL EQUINOX. So, now you begin to understand my dates of the prophecies. December 24th is the SCORPION on the EAST. The MOUNTAIN GOAT CAPRICORN appears on the NORTHERN sky in late September transitioning the Galactic Virgin into the Libra sign. Now, I hope, you understand the September 17th date when the GOAT, the 'Devil' appears in the northern sky. By September 23rd, in the middle of his body we see that from a Mountain Goat he transformed into a FISH. It is a strange mermaid. That is when the Water Tsunami came at the eruption of the Orion Nebula black hole. From the bottom of the ocean where the fish lives – the tsunami ran up to the top of the mountains, where the mountain goat lives." – Santa was serious about these comical animals.

I was intensely studying the pictures to be able to ask questions and finally to understand these extremely important cosmic mysteries.

"So, I think I understand the bottom picture, … the Scorpion is the December Christmas, and the Goat is the end of the September Tsunami, … but, what about the Bear … and the Harp being played by the Donkey?" – I asked.

"That's easy." – Saint Nick proclaimed. I looked at Eva with disbelief. She made a grimace that was neutral as far as I could interpret it. I was not sure if she made that face for me or against me. Well, I don't care - there was nothing 'easy' on this picture. A few idiotic animals explaining the cosmic mysteries of the Earth is 'not easy'. Common Santa! – I was having these raging thoughts in my mind. Although, it cannot be that idiotic if the Democratic Party picked the DONKEY as their symbol, then it is significant. If the donkey was present in the barn at Christ's birth, it is significant. Okay, I started analyzing. If the BEAR holds that pillar, then it is the POLAR NORTH of the geo-dynamo. The HARP – LYRE star constellation has the VEGA star that is the HAWK Horus, which symbolizes the MAGNETIC NORTH. But why would the DONKEY be involved there. Why would that stubborn donkey be there even at the Christmas Barn at Christ Birth? Jesus Christ was not born, yet during these times 4,600 – 5,000 years ago when the FIRST city of UR was established in Babylonia.

"So, the DONKEY is the same Astronomical Donkey in Sumer 5,000 years ago – that we have seen 3,000 years later at Christ birth?" – I inquired with a shy voice knowing I hit on something.

"Excellent observation!" – Saint Nick burst out in a loud approval. "Now, you are thinking!"

"So, all of these animal symbols are just Astronomy that marks the time of the year in the sky. Will we learn why the ancient viziers picked a certain animal to represent a certain cosmic event?" – I asked.

"The two DONKEY stars are in the shaft of the Cancer CRAB star constellation. This is a sea CRAB that walks sideways on the beach. This represents the axis shift. This is present on every continent from the Egyptians to the Mayans, Incas, Greeks, Romans. The Egyptians use the CRAB, which the Egyptologists call the Dung BEETLE, but it is the CANCER star constellation. If it was so universally known to our creation legend makers than how come, we don't know it? ... Look at the book on your bookshelf from Maurice Cotterell." – He smiled and he put his hand through the wall. His arm extended over 10 feet to reach inside the house to grab the book. 'Why did he asked me before to fetch any book for him when he could do that trick on his own' – I wondered.

"Here it is." – He pulled the book across the wall to show us. "This is the story of Viracocha, the CRAB god of the Peruvians. This is not any different than the CRAB that the ancient Greeks talk about with ORION in their classical mythology. It is not any different than this Peruvian Inca CRAB god." – Santa explained as he showed the book.

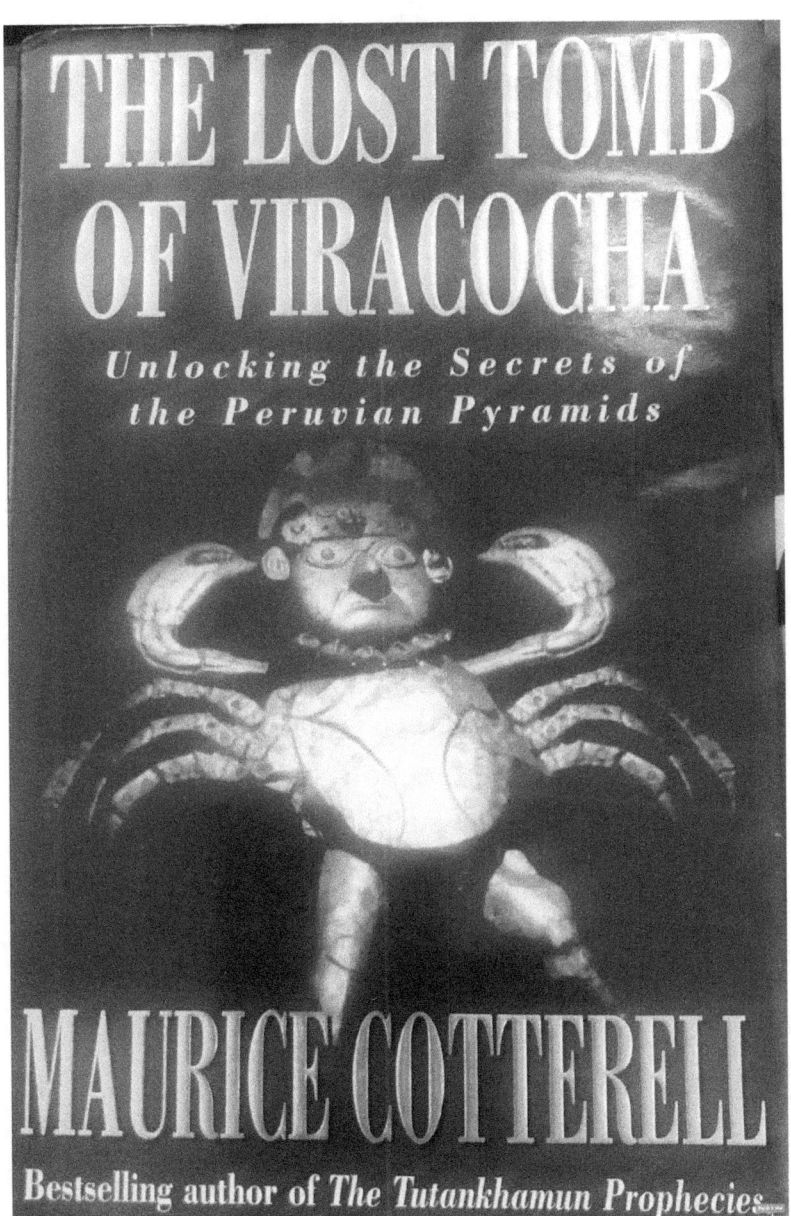

THE LOST TOMB OF VIRACOCHA

Unlocking the Secrets of the Peruvian Pyramids

MAURICE COTTERELL

Bestselling author of *The Tutankhamun Prophecies*

"Why the CRAB Viracocha is a 'god'?" – I asked.

"So, this is how I see it now." – Eva cut in. "The unseen cosmic force, the Voice of the Almighty God that comes periodically to disrupt the idyllic harmony of Nature – as much as it is needed – creates a scenario that needs to be explained in a hidden manner using Astronomy. This is brilliant if you want to keep secrets from your people. Nobody will equate a Crab with the most powerful force of Nature!" – Eva was elated as she untangled the enigmas.

"It is pure Astronomy. There was a good reason why the leaders kept this a secret from the masses. I will not go into details right now, but the Two Donkeys hidden in the body of the Crab was a good design." – Santa stated with confidence.

"Would You please explain." – I politely asked, which surprised me because my conscious mind was upset and confused. I was ready to scream.

"This is the date March 26th, … when Re-Creation happened. When you look up the Astronomy, you will notice that on March 26th looking up North toward Polaris one can see the CANCER constellation on the northern view. The TWO STARS in the shaft of the Cancer star constellation are called the Northern DONKEY and the Southern DONKEY. This is where the TWO PILLARS of the Earth's Geo-dynamo united and later separated. Like a stubborn donkey, stop and go." – He smiled, knowing that it would be too much even for us.

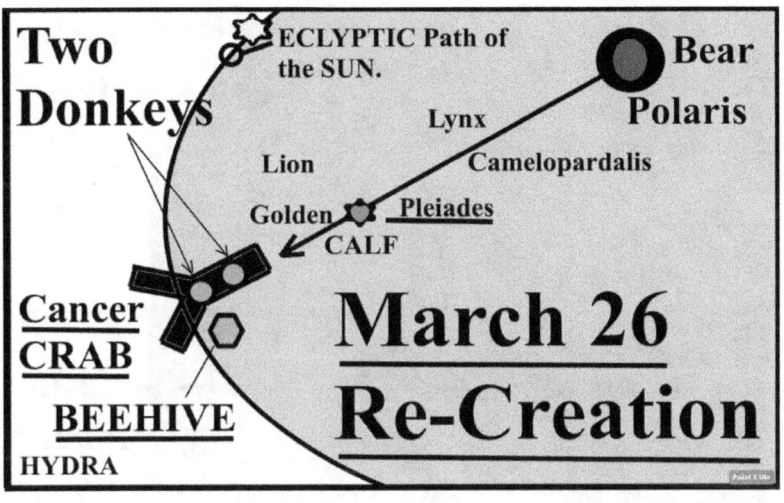

"So, all these star constellations surrounding the March 26th date has a specific meaning?" – I asked.

"Exactly! The CANCER CRAB or in Egypt the Dung Beetle is the one who walks sideways or who rolls the dung or our globe backwards. That represent the AXIS SHIFT. The Beehive reminds of angry bees flying out of the hive representing CYGNUS and the Orion black hole eruptions on

March 26th. The line cuts through the Pleiades heart of the Bull or the Golden Calf – and now you are bringing in the shamanic and biblical knowledge together." – the Old Man of Winter was exhaustive.

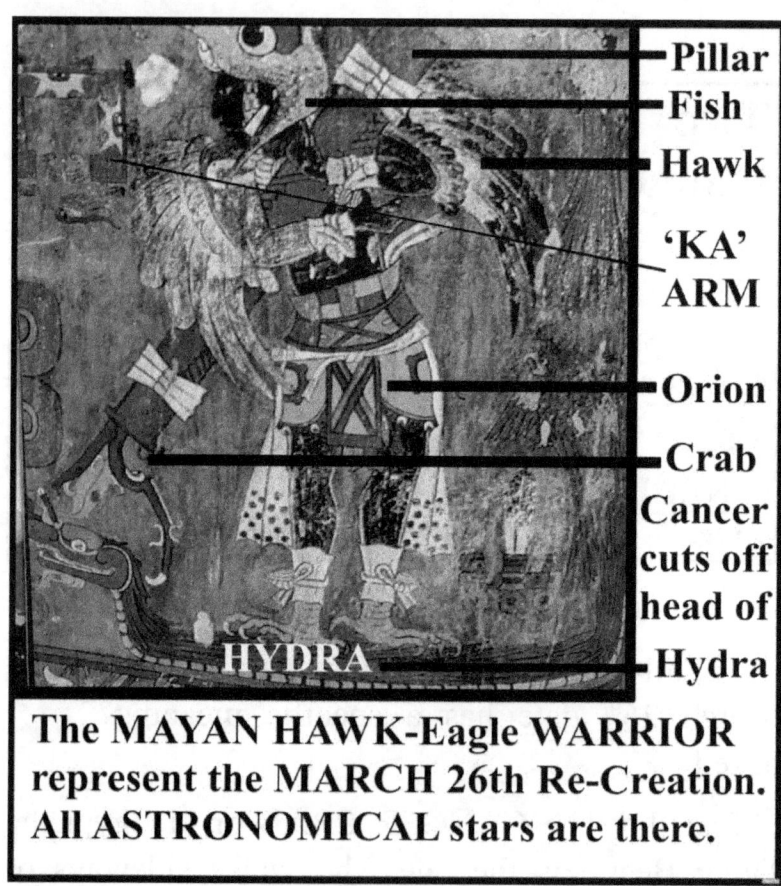

Pillar
Fish
Hawk

'KA'
ARM

Orion

Crab
Cancer
cuts off
head of
Hydra

HYDRA

The MAYAN HAWK-Eagle WARRIOR represent the MARCH 26th Re-Creation. All ASTRONOMICAL stars are there.

"Okay, how come the Mayans with their calendar did not show this same Astronomy." – I wondered.

"I am glad you asked. ... As matter-of-fact to be honest – I put this taught into your brain to be able to make a point." – Santa Claus pulled up a Mayan picture of a warrior who seemingly represented all the Astronomy one would want to see about March 26th. "Go find the Crab, Hydra, Hawk, Orion, etc."

"This is like learning a new language. A language of Astronomy and Cosmology. When the ancient star priest made up the holy books, how did they expect us to solve this riddle that is more difficult than college level algebra. ... And because one cosmic event is drawn up so many different way - with so many different astronomical animals, one cannot decipher all the intended meanings." – I huffed and puffed. "There are not even animals in the natural story. It is a black hole eruption causing upheaval." – I was a little frustrated.

"I understand your frustration. Almost no normal human on the face of the Earth would be able to solve these riddles unless they receive some help from above. That is what's happening now." – Santa stated.

"A stubborn Donkey, a Crab cutting off the Head of Hydra, a toreador sword through the shoulder blade of the Bull, that is the Pleiades ... all representing Re-Creation?" – I asked with surprise.

"That is a lot. Impossible. ... Did you both notice earlier the staff that the Polaris BEAR holds, goes through the shoulder blade of the BULL in Babylonia? That is the Pleiades! It is also in the Bible in the Book of Job." – Saint Nick stated it like this was kindergarten level knowledge that everybody should understand. "Okay, this was difficult, I admit." – Santa finally apologized.

Eva and I both agreed. "Tough beyond belief, you can say that again." – I complained.

"You want to live - you got to learn. You stop learning, you will die. ... So, let me show you one more picture so you can see the same thing with different animals." – Santa offered. "Egyptian boat left to right - first 4 years."

Trapezium of ORION NEBULA	EYE ERUPTS 12-25-21 Sept. 23-22		MARCH 26, '26 The Axis Shift RE-CREATION

ORION

"This is again the first four years of the climate changes. The EYE eruption from Orion in the first column is the December event on the left. Then the first 'person' from left to right after that is the September event. That secretly gave the hidden cosmic base for Rosh Hashanah. The fourth 'creature', is the Ram (Amon-Ra / Sol-Amon) at the end of March 3 ½ years later in the Aries sign." – Santa explained. "These are the things you have to recognize to understand the creation mythologies. You will be tested at the end." – Santa stated. "You must recognize the astronomical animals!"

"I wish that they would only use one animal for one event or one holiday." – I said. Eva nodded.

"Way too many scenarios with different animals and heroes that mean the same thing." – Eva agreed.

"I agree. There is one more picture that will show you two the same concept of the first four years from Egypt." – Santa Claus revealed with enthusiasm. – "Right to left. The Eye erupts first."

The First FOUR Years (R to L) Paint X lite

"See, the fourth year here is the Sekhmet Lioness, not the Ram. That is why it is so confusing." – I complained aloud again.

"… and it means the same cosmic event. You will have to know the Astronomy from all different directions with all existing concepts. It is not just Astronomy, but also Cosmology." – Santa insisted.

"I agree with Willy, … the more pictures you show us Santa, the more confusing it becomes." – my wife came to my defense.

"You will be able to tell if you begin to understand the Astronomy and the Cosmology as you read the creation mythologies. When you read those stories, you need to look up the Astronomy of the season and look at the Dendera Zodiac to understand that a Lioness is at the end of March, passed the Golden Calf – rather than in August when you would expect the Leo sign to dominate. You are both capable to learn these creation mythologies and you will understand the science behind it. I promise." – Santa answered back. I had a strange feeling that I needed to cough, like I was choking, but it passed fast. I felt numb in my brain, like someone just gave me too much something, may be sedatives to calm me down. I would be calm if these astronomical meanings would not keep changing every time, I look at them. I felt empty and dumb.

"We can learn these, I hope so! We will learn all the nuances until we get it." – Eva sighed. "It seems that the Astronomy and Cosmology unites all religions." Her sentences were echoing in my ears like when someone records a phone conversation. I just wanted to sleep.

3.

The Prophecy

All the conversations that we had with Santa Claus seemed like happened so fast that it was over in a few minutes, although it had to last hours. As we were standing in front of the Golden Chariot, I asked Santa if he could outline the prophecies a little better, so I can think about it and prepare for it. He looked at me with wondering eyes.

"In the center of the Universe sits the KING. He is God. He is physically smaller than an atom and electro-magnetically and spiritually larger than the whole Universe. He continually releases resonation from his Holy Mouth and that is how He creates and maintains. Spiral 5 & 5 unites to 6. His words speak great wisdom. He says the one verse that holds up the world, that is why we call it (H)-UN-i-VERSE. We see that Huge Black Hole in the vicinity of the tip of Cepheus, the HEAD star constellation that is next to Polaris. The name of the star is Er Raj, 'THE KING' or 'THE SHEPHERD'. Now you both understand why we call God the King or the Shepherd. Right, the 'Lord is my Shepherd'. – He looked up to the sky with reverence.

"We know this Almighty God well?" – Eva asked.

"You did not think that was known to your 'simple-minded' Biblical forefathers?" – he smiled mysteriously. "Then His Voice, the resonation reaches our Milky Way and the 4 important black holes, first the Sagittarius A in center of the Milky Way". He thought for a second. - "Then this resonation reaches the Orion Nebula, Cygnus X-1 and X-3 every 5,786 years. The first is the Orion Nebula." – Santa sighed. "The Great Hunter."

"That is where He is. In the Orion Nebula black hole?" – Eva nodded toward Bes. The old man nodded back in agreement.

"He is still a baby." – Eva joked.

"You got that one right!" – Santa responded quick.

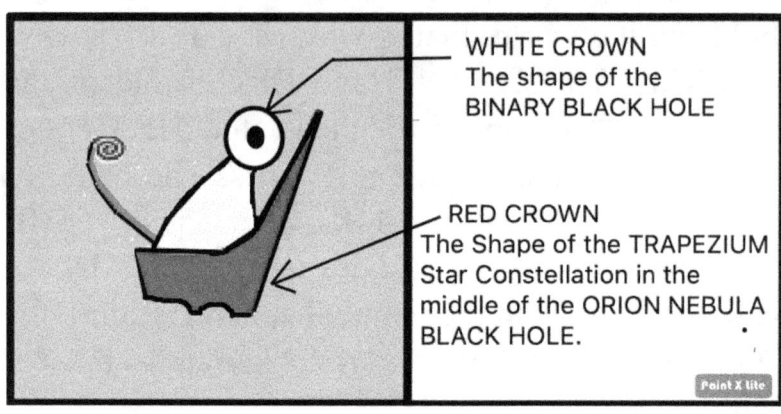

"Look at his Red Crown and White Crown on Bes and on the Pharaohs' heads". – Santa pointed out.

"The White Crown is the shape of a Binary black hole. Look it up at NASA. So, the White Crown of Bes is to say – I represent the Binary Black Hole. Then the Red Crown represents the Trapezium star constellation where the Orion Nebula Black Hole is. Trapezium is positioned in the Orion Nebula and defines where the black hole positioned. Think of it as God veins and arteries supply the Universe where the force travels." – the old man explained. "Soon we will learn why the hawk-headed Horus wears these same crowns, who represents the

MAGNETIC NORTH axis of the Earth. The Black Hole of Orion is connected to the Magnetic North of the Earth and controls the climate cycles." – Santa knew so much and understood the Cosmic Forces. It sounded scientific, but totally alien to the teachings we received in our religious upbringings.

"Let me show you the picture of the Milky Way Galaxy as shown by our scientists at NASA, ESA and other great institutions. On this picture you will see the huge Supermassive BLACK HOLE in the Center of our Galaxy. The second largest black hole is in the CYGNUS star constellation complex. It is the Northern Cross. Now, you start understanding what Christ wanted to teach us by the example of the CROSS?" – Santa was excited.

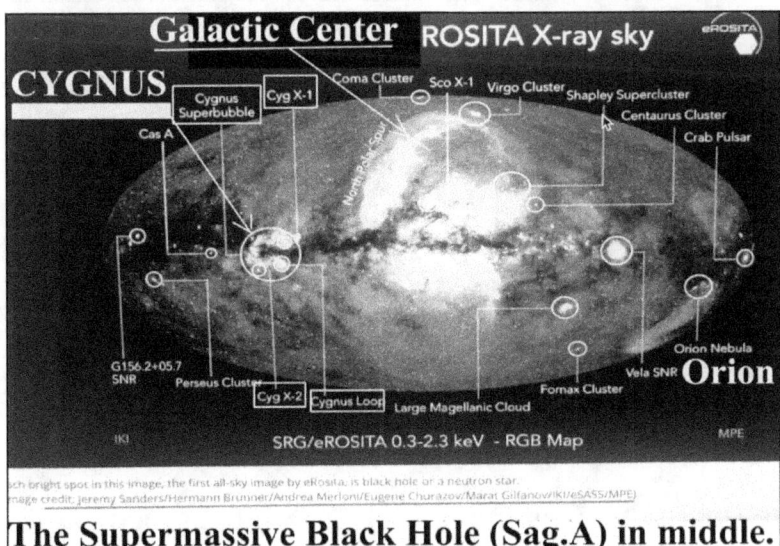

The Supermassive Black Hole (Sag.A) in middle. CYGNUS 2nd largest. Orion is the closest B.H.

"These are the positions of the largest Black Holes?" – I asked knowing the answer already.

"You have to know these black holes, also the ones in the Center of the Universe, then you both have to know where the markers are for the Polar North and the Magnetic North, - and how they interact with these black hole power houses. How they cause the Axis Shift of the Earth's geo-dynamo. That's all." – Santa rattled off the short list that we were responsible for.

"… and know the Virgin?" – I offered. Santa nodded affirmatively. "She stands on the left side of the Galactic Center." – I concluded.

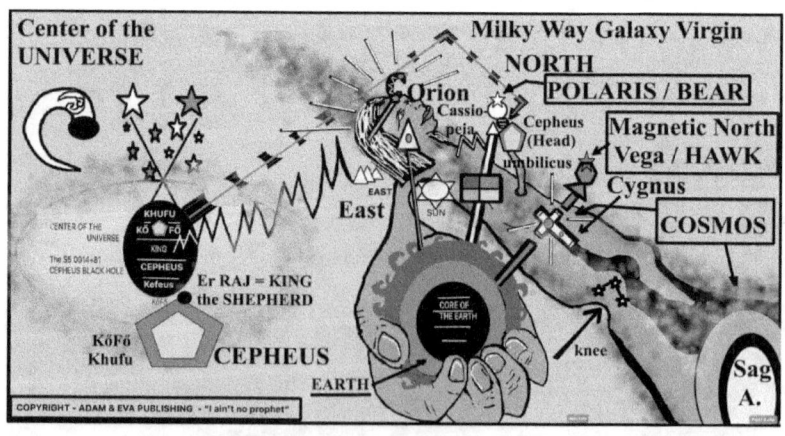

"Learn this Cosmic model." – Santa agreed.

"Otherwise, we die?" – I tried to joke with the old man. He looked up and nothing but unconditional love and the yearning to teach the truth was emanating from his lapis lazuli blue eyes.

"Yes. But I am trying to teach you something more important than one's life - without the fear of death. It is the UNIVERSAL TRUTH!" - Saint Nick stated in a soft non-threatening voice.

"But you are only joking with the 'death'?" – Eva asked trying to get a reassuring wink.

"Not joking." – Santa reaffirmed his earlier promise. "Death is new life. You learn here or die."

"That's messed up!" – I stated with a hint of anger.

"It is too late for you two to go back now. You have come too far." Saint Nicholas affirmed.

"This is just so alien to our minds." – I begged.

"You almost can't go back to live as normal human beings - after this much knowledge. More reasons to learn it." – Santa was confident.

"You will be tested on this knowledge and more, so let's begin absorbing it. Go back and look at the picture. On the left-hand side, you can see the Center of the Universe, it is represented by Cepheus. In it sits the mythologically largest black hole. We almost, cannot see 12 billion light years away even with our best instruments, but this enormous size black hole can be seen right at the top of the CEPHEUS star constellation, next to the star named 'Er Raj', the 'King' or the 'Shepherd'. Now, I hope you both begin to understand why we call Him the King of the Universe or our Shepherd. In the right corner of the picture is the Center of our Milky Way Galaxy. It is marked by the Sagittarius A black hole. Going left from the Center toward the middle of the picture is the part of our Milky Way Galaxy we call the Galactic Virgin." – He paused. – "Can you both see that?" – Santa asked. "That is Christ Celestial Virgin Mother and Mary is the virgin human mother." He stated.

"We can see it just fine." – Eva spoke for both of us. "Two mothers, huh, … we have two mothers, one biological and one adapted." - she smiled.

"Now, you can then identify the closest runaway black hole to Earth in the Brain of the Galactic Virgin. That is the Orion Nebula. This is the first Cosmic Secret." – Santa was methodical.

"Thus, this is the reason Michelangelo's painting of the cross section of the brain behind God in the 'Creation of Adam' picture. The Vatican knew and still knows the cosmic secrets." – Eva concluded with surprise.

"Exactly! I might still be able to make prophets out of you two!" – Santa joked around. – "Maybe." – He winked. I did not think it was funny with the promise of death, but for now it seemed that we learn and pass our tests. Santa believed in us. That was an interesting feeling. They always asked us in the past to see if 'we believe in Santa Claus', this was the first time that it was important that 'Santa believed in us.'

"Coming out of the Galactic Center is the ORION CYGNUS ARM. Your beautiful Earth is on the extension of that on the ORION CYGNUS ARM. That is why the first letter 'A' of the Egyptian hieroglyphic alphabet is the ARM = the letter 'A'. Well, I bet no Egyptologist taught you that. This is how it has been done for 100,000 of years." – Santa was motivated to hand us more knowledge.

"Nobody told us that." – I complained.

"The whole Egyptian hieroglyphic alphabet is built on this cosmic knowledge that I am presenting to you." – Santa handed us another secret we did not know. "When you both make it out of the kindergarten of the Cosmic Prophet School then I or someone else will teach you the alphabet to such a detail – you would not imagine existed. It is a promise." – Saint Nick knew so much he was hard to follow.

"In her hand the Galactic Virgin is holding the geo-dynamo of the Earth. The Magnetic North is pointing to the Vega Star in the Harp Lyre star constellation. It is the SWOOPING HAWK, the Egyptian HORUS. Naturally, it is about 90 degrees to the plain of the Solar System. Then the Polar North points to the POLARIS. It sits on the EQUATOR, which runs on the ORION CYGNUS ARM. So, basically, the Equator of the Earth ends up in the Orion star constellation. We need to know these scientific facts to solve the Cosmic Secrets." – Santa was serious about the subject. Eva and I were a little bit overwhelmed with all that information.

"How come this is not written down in the Bible, the Torah and other holy books." – I asked. "If it is this important, it should be there." – I insisted.

"Ho, ho, hooo!" – Santa Claus was bellying out a big laugh from his skinny body. It was not as impressive as the ones he could truly do as a morbidly obese red-faced Nordic old man. Sometimes, I think a voice box is better equipped if the person is overweight. – "I am glad you brought it up. You can read the Torah, or you can read the Bible, it is in it. … Okay, when you have a chance - read Book of Job, Chapter 9, verses 4 – 9. There you will find the mention that the Orion is one of the constellations that can remove mountains from their places. ... Just read it. Everything I state is biblical, but it takes a lot of digging and connecting." – Santa Claus seemed to know the answers to every question we would pose to him.

"I will read it. Is it a prophecy?" – I wondered.

"So, you want to know the prophecy, before you learn the details?" – he wondered. "The Book of Job is part of the prophecy. It mentions that it is the ORION, PLEIADES AND THE BEAR that will cause mountains to move out of their places. I already started on the path to make you understand that statement. We will give you more details so you can feel good about what I am teaching you." – Santa explained.

"Yes. I want to know the prophecy." – I was honest.

"Me too!" – Eva chimed in. She was upbeat, although we did not know the whole story, yet.

"Before I teach the two of you everything you need to know in this makeshift prophet school, I would like to provide you with the TIMELINE OF THE PROPHECY." – the old Man of Winter stated.

He pulled out an old appearing yellow paper from the inside of his red tunic and handed it to me. He apparently did not know that I needed reading glasses, especially at night.

"Read it out loud, so Eva can hear it, too!" – Santa Claus pleaded with me. He did not care about my reading glasses that I did not have. "Once, you know this prophecy, it will save your lives and the ones around you. If you ignore it, you will die either a happy death of ignorance or a miserable one. One can only prepare for what he knows. If you want to win you have to know what to prepare for, what is coming and in what order. You cannot build an Ark like Noah did if all the trees burnt up." – Santa Claus was making good sense, but we were too excited to listen to his reasoning. We just wanted to hear the prophecy and know what to expect as the worst-case scenario.

"We want to hear the prophecy." – Eva and I were honest about our over-flowing curiosity. Santa Claus will make us prophets for real.

"Okay, here is the timeline of the Prophecy." – Saint Nick turn to us. "Read" – he looked at me.

RED CLOUD PROPHECY

Station 1. The ORION NEBULA black hole will

erupt around December 25th, 2021. The Conception of the Son. The Last 14 years begins.

Station 2. The ORION NEBULA black hole will erupt again around September 17th – 23rd, 2022. This can bring miracles, or it can result in a large earthquake and an enormous tsunami. This is the Birth of Bes - 9 months after Christmas. This is the time of Rosh Hashanah, Atonement.

Station 3. The 2nd and 3rd events right after the birth. Flying Pig. Frogs. Halloween.

Station 4. The eruption of Cygnus X-3 black hole on March 26th, 2026. Amazing long life and peace on Earth, … or a miserable Axis shift with the Destruction of Humanity. Everything burns to ashes. It is humanity's moral choice. It will be the Day of Re-Creation! Ten years later we can have the

Deluge of Noah. 2026 will be the 10 years Flood warning!

"Nobody knows the hour." – I muttered as a good Christian. Santa looked at me lovingly.

"I agree. The day, week, month, or the exact year should suffice." – His eyes were twinkling. "Although, we even know the hour when Orion is in the East on Christmas Eve." - He grinned.

"Can I say something?" – Eva raised her right arm with her second and third fingers pointing up, as if she was still in elementary school.

"Certainly, you may." – Santa gave permission as he was covering up Bes with the lion skin on the seat of the chariot. The Red Hyena pulled under the blanket and poked her / his head out. She was cross-eyed. She looked at the old man as if it would understand everything that was being said.

"You know Santa, in our search for writing our last book the God's Generator, we found these two dates you mentioned; September 17 and March 26, as the two dates when the Washington Monument throws a shadow on the door of the Congress." – Eva paused theatrically.

"Correct. That is a small part of the reasons why we chose the two of you to become the pupils of this prophet school." – Santa Claus explained. "You already miles ahead of others who we considered, ... but you are still so far away." – He said it almost as he would be singing a catchy melody. "You have to learn to connect myths to science."

"Like knowing the FURNACE of Orion – as you climb through the CHIMNEY Santa, I guess?" - Eva joked. "... and you live at Polar North."

"No guessing, I guess. God's Universe is perfect, it is designed with accuracy." – he reassured her. "What we need is that open mind, truthfulness, praise for the One God King of the Universe - yes, ... but guessing, no!" – the Man of Winter from the Polar North was holding his staff from the side of the chariot. The staff ended in a spiral design and Santa was holding it in a 23.4 degrees angle, just as our Earth would have it on the Polar North.

"Willy, you wanted to have an outline. You need visual. I provided you with that early on, so both of you can prepare for the immense learning that will follow on this journey. Pull out your Cosmic Law I Pod that I gave you. We will begin with the SACRED ROCK that maintains life on Earth. That is the only rock the wizards need to know about. All other rocks are there to throw you off the path." -

He invited us to sit in the Golden Chariot drawn by the Seven Reindeers. He sat next to Bes with his back to the driver seat. We were lucky to get the back seat that faced ahead.

"The first lesson is to understand that everything we use as garment, colors, animal symbols all have very exact meaning in the sky. You have to find Perseus, Taurus Bull, Orion." – Santa reassured. "We should get going now."

A male Goat walked up to the Chariot standing as a man with three little goat kiddies following in his footsteps. They easily jumped up to the front seat, the adult goat who behaved as a human comfortably checked the rein and decided it was time to dart off.

"Station ZERO" – Santa dictated the direction to Kapella Kaprikorn, the charioteer. He nodded imperceptibly. The chariot took off quieter than a fancy drone. I noticed the houses, the streets and the lights from our neighborhood disappearing under us. Everything got progressively smaller as we accelerated up the pitch back sky with flickering stars. I looked over to Eva who was petting the red hyena. I certainly expected to pull some G's, but the flight felt very magical. I noticed that I had no fear of heights for some strange reasons. We were making sharper turns and falling out was not even on my mind.

"Where are we going exactly?" – Eva asked softly, not to wake up the spotted red hyena who herself was a genetic miracle of some sort. We did not know, yet. It was transforming from female to male.

"The first place we will visit is Station Zero, where we outline the structure of the Universe, Milky Way, the Solar System and the Earth's geo-dynamo. We will be meeting at least 12 members of the whispering team after that." – Santa informed us.

"Whispering?" – Eva chuckled. "How anybody hear them if they whisper?" - Cutie Eva insisted. Santa smiled. He turned around and pointed at a dome shaped glass castle in the distance.

"That is where we are going.: - he pointed to the far distance. As we got closer, the shape of the building looked like the liberty bell but appeared to be of thin clear glass. It seemed flexible and pliable.

"Here we are." Santa stood up after we reached the docking side of a UFO shaped structure that was several houses wide on the western side. There was an interesting soft greenish grayish silver metal floor. Eva and I stayed sitting to see what was proper behavior? Santa walked out followed by Bes, the red hyena, the white dog and then the goats. Kapella Kaprikorn, or as we got to know him 'KK' the leading goat who drove the Golden Chariot, pointed to us to follow the entourage. The little goats came followed us and soon disappeared into one of the rooms of the metal structure. We went through the center hallway and reached the liberty bell glass bubble house. It had an opening, but Santa stopped before he entered in. All his team stopped behind him. Santa Claus waved us closer, and we were totally surprised that the glass house appeared to be without any furniture, walls, decorations. As matter of fact, it was totally empty.

"First, it will be strange to walk on air, but we are at the Edge of Space, the edge of atmosphere where gravity does not play a part. You will not sink or fall. You follow me. You can pretend to sit down, and a spiritual chair or desk will appear. There are no earthly materials on the East side of this bubble, but anything you think of can appear out of thin air." – He stated it with serious confidence and then burst into a laugh seeing our scared looks.

Eva and I looked at each other and she pretended to be excited. I did not have to pretend, I was scared.

"We do this neutral territory so we shall not compromise the integrity of the spirits that will appear to us for teaching purposes." – Santa declared. "Who's gonna go first?" – Santa looked at both of us with an encouraging stare.

"I will go first." – Eva bravely walked into the bubble house with invisible glass floor. I did not follow quickly enough. I was contemplating.

Santa looked at me with starry eyes. I was busy staring at Eva's adventures. She walked up to an area and a living room opened, with everything one would need for comfort and communication. "She has a great imagination for creating a home, doesn't she?" – the old man smiled.

'That she certainly does." – I agreed.

"Your turn." – he extended his right arm toward the perceived opening. To me it still looked like I walk across a glass door and step into nothingness, then I will likely fall toward Earth until I disintegrate. Large fat droplets then littering Earth. Knowing that there were no other options, I entered the abyss. Nothing weird happened. I was walking into a large beautifully decorated living room. Eva was already preparing some coffee and cookies. Santa was walking behind me.

"Please, go ahead and drink the coffee if it relaxes you. Nothing physical exist here accept what our imagination prepared for us. Sit down and relax." – Claus encouraged me.

"Who is the first Egyptian teacher you would like to see?" – the old man asked. – "Cross your fingers to make it happen."

"I would personally enjoy getting an update from Thoth." I proclaimed crossing my fingers.

"Yeah, that is the Egyptian Greco-Roman deity Thoth Trismegistus or Hermes Mercury, right?" – Eva chimed in. Santa nodded. "Why him if I may ask?" – Santa inquired.

"Well, most major religion credit Him as their founder from Egypt to Persia. Judeo-Christians and Islam was influenced by it. Most spiritual tradition, mysticism and even the Scientific Revolution gave Him credits. He believed in the 'prisca theologia', the 'one true religion of God'." - I admitted.

"I am very happy you two decided on the Egyptian Thoth, who is also known as the Greek HERMES Trismegistus and the Roman Mercury." – Santa smiled and quickly disappeared in thin air.

"You called me in. Here I am. I am who I am." – Thoth's voice ringed in right as soon as we thought of him. He appeared at the East wall of the bubble. He was outside, but there appeared to be no wall between us. He walked closer and a golden throne appeared beneath him as he was sitting back down. I was thinking, how nice it would be if we could just live like that. Imagine something and it would appear where it supposed to be. He was about 8 feet tall with a human body and an ibis head dress. His traditional Egyptian garment seemed expansive and very colorful with gold inlets. Thoth made a few circles with his arms and expansive looking antique furniture appeared in the large palace room we were now sitting in. In seconds the whole palace transformed into a place that even Cleopatra would envy. Once he felt comfortable and royally positioned on the throne, he motioned with eloquence to open the floor for questioning.

"Ask any relevant questions and I will answer it honestly." – Thoth opened to us.

"God's Blessings to you Thoth! Can I ask personal sounding questions? Are you an Egyptian stork who brings the baby?" – Eva asked with an innocent voice.

"For the historical appearance I am the bird, but truthfully I am nothing that I look like here. This is my mythological persona. So, for now, I am definitely the stork who brings the baby in the position of Mercury and much more." – he laughed out loud. – "Ask your questions about that."

"Why did you decide to become a Stork, … ibis, 'benu', I mean? Ben is the Hebrew 'son'. Could not an eagle bring the baby?" – Eva further inquired.

"Every animal, every bird carries an important character that we use to give the cosmic-earthly event a flavor." – Thoth proclaimed.

I was looking at Eva to see if she was satisfied with the explanation. Both her and I had more questions.

"What are those characters of the stork?" – Eva wondered. "I mean for the cosmic birth. What animal characteristics you have to possess to represent the Cosmic Birth?" – my wife asked.

"When the Cosmic Baby Bes was re-born by the black hole eruption, first a small then later a larger tsunami happened on Earth. Water was standing on the ground. Not deep, not everywhere, but enough for lot of frogs to exist. Like in the biblical plagues." – Thoth looked up. We were enthusiastically nodding and encouraged him with our looks to continue. - "Storks eat frogs!" – He said it with a straight face and seeing our confused look He burst out in an infectious laugh. "Taste like chicken." – we smiled at the joke.

"Okay?!" – we looked at each other.

"The stork stands in the shallow water. We tied the effects of the Cosmic Births to the bird who eats frogs and stands in shallow water. Stand on

ONE LEG, as the EARTH will stand on one leg for a short while when the axis shift happens." – Thoth explained it patiently. "Too complicated?"

"Complex but makes perfect sense. So, Bes is the cosmic baby that you will deliver again?" – Eva's question was light and playful. She peered into the direction of the sky where Bes was likely resting.

"Bes is the Baby." – Thoth answered with an even voice. Then three and a half year later it will be the Lamb of God." – he remained cool and collected. – "This has been going on for hundreds of thousands of years. At least." – Thoth reassured us.

"Well, the biblical teaching talks about the frogs and the lotus and a whole bunch of other things. Is it the same cosmic event?" – I was curious.

"Yes. Moses and Christ were the last ones teaching it. The cosmic event was referenced back to 5,786 years ago but the events were taught as a nation building religious wisdom." – Thoth added. – "Be 100 % sure that it is not any human birth we celebrate, but it is the human deities, prophets and messengers who celebrate Bes' birth. You will learn that from several different sources on this journey." – Thoth reassured us. - "It is never humans we talk about! Think allegorically!"

"We are not afraid to learn anything." – Eva said with true enthusiasm. "Plus, we want to live." – she looked over at me. I gave her the 'both thumbs' up.

"You will live on that side or on this side, might as well do something useful." – Thoth stated.

"How come you are so popular with all cultures?" – I inquired politely.

"Okay, my most known work is translated into multiple languages. Initially, it was written down in the Smaragd Tablets that most of you might know better as the Emerald Tablets. Let me introduce my basic teachings and then I will explain it in detail - so you can pass your tests and live on the physical plane for a little longer." – Thoth offered.

A Universal Truth is ONE that be true in every system, large and small. Unless you understand what happens in the Universe, Galaxy, you will not understand the Sun and Earth. You will not understand how a new protoplanet or a new star is formed." – Thoth stated.

"I will outline my teachings about the Earth's geo-dynamo and the Sun, and we will show you how it is true for the Universe. Here is my short teaching on the subject point by point." – Thoth exclaimed.

"First, understand that the Universe, the galaxies, the Sun, the Earth – all work as DYNAMOS. One WIRE of this dynamo is driven from a larger magnetic source and the other wire is tied to a lesser, but equally important source. For example, the GALACTIC ARM'S PLAIN controls the POLAR AXIS, and the SUN SOLAR PLAIN stabilizes the MAGNETIC NORTH. The Galaxy is much bigger than the Sun." – He stated with confidence.

"This system is universal and turns all dynamos. It works from, the largest dynamo of the Universe, to lesser and lesser size galaxies and solar systems, down to the dynamo of the Earth. This is the most basic understanding. As you noticed yourselves, people do not know the least amount of astronomical information about the details of the Earth's geo-dynamo." – Thoth explained. "Let us look at the Teachings of The Emerald Tablets."

THE EMERALD TABLET OF HERMES papyrus appeared on the wall, and it read the following.

1 This is the truth, the whole truth and nothing but the truth.

2 AS BELOW, SO ABOVE; and AS ABOVE SO BELOW. With this knowledge alone you may work miracles.

3 Since ALL THINGS exist in and emanate from the ONE who is the ultimate Cause, so all things are derived from this SOURCE.

4 Here in our Solar System the SUN is the father - and the Moon is the mother. (52 years Generations!)

5 The Wind carries this unseen POWER in its belly, and the Earth is its nurse and guardian.

6 It is the FATHER and MOTHER of ALL THINGS.

7 a, Here on Earth its STRENGHT, its POWER remains one and undivided.

7 b, Earth must be separated from Fire, the subtle from the dense,

8 It arises from the Earth and descends from heaven; it gathers to itself the STRENGHT of things above and things below.

9 By understanding this ONE thing, the glory of the whole world can be yours and all obscurity and misunderstanding will avoid you.

10 Its FORCE is ABOVE ALL FORCE. It vanquishes every subtle thing and penetrates every solid thing.

11 So EVERYTHING that the World contains was created by this FORCE.

12 From this FORCE are born manifold wonders, all adaptations by the MODE revealed here.

13 It is for this reason that I am called HERMES TRISMEGISTUS, for I possess the THREEFOLD essentials of the philosophy of the Universal Creation.

14 This is the sum-total of the WORK OF THE SUN.

Eva and I looked at each other in utter amazement. Hermes Trismegistus Mercury Thoth looked up and seemed satisfied with the wisdom.

"You understand it or do I need to provide explanation." – Thoth asked. Our face told the truth.

"Let me give you the answer and show you pictures so you will understand it. … The ONE FORCE that I am talking about is the ELETRO-MAGNETIC POWER in the CENTER OF THE UNIVERSE! – Thoth began his explanation.

"It is huge dynamo which is originating from a source less than a cell size. It is where the unseen POWER of GOD is hidden, which holds up the whole Universe. You must understand that God is not flesh, it can make flesh, but in its wholeness, cannot be made flesh or will die. It cannot become flesh and then live forever because the flesh disintegrates. He can send His daughters and sons, but He remains the unseen sacred Force of Electro-Magnetism that contains all knowledge. He is both the MALE and FEMALE principles in ONE. He creates from the ELECTRO-MAGNETIC SPIRAL PAIR. The interactions of the large MALE SPIRAL and a large FEMALE SPIRAL creates the infinite numbers of forms. The SPIRAL breaks into 5 parts. That is why so many nations will carry the FIVE-pointed pentagram stars on their flags. That is why the Pentagon building is five sided. All you have to do is to look at your fingers and toes to count this recurring five on our own bodies." – Thoth explained with eternal patience.

"I would like to add something here, if I may, Thoth." – a different voice filled the air. Eva and I both looked. It was an American who walked in from the 1800th centuries. First, we thought he had to be one of the Founding Fathers, but he really did not resemble either of the Presidents. He was a founding father of a different order.

"Albert. Join us in this important conversation. I might have stated something that required your presence." – Thoth spoke politely. The man was Albert Pike the Founder of Freemasonry of the Ancient and Accepted Scottish Rite, Southern Jurisdiction. A giant amongst the Patriots searching for Beauty, Equality, Strength, and

Wisdom for all people. His long hair and beard made him look like a mountain man who dressed up for the audience.

"If you are true seekers of the Grand Word and you want to possess the Great Secret, then you are all looking for the Philosophal Stone. It cannot be exposed to the atmosphere or the gaze of the Profane. But for you I can tell that this largest stone is inside the Center of the Universe and our largest on Earth is inside Mother Earth as part of the geo-dynamo. It is the most amazing part of the Great Work of the Creator, the Grand Architect of the Universe, the Infinite Intelligence. The Sun and the Moon of the Alchemists concur in perfecting and giving stability to the Philosophal Stone. They correspond to the two columns of the Temple, Jachin and Boaz." – He slowly looked up at us to see the facial reactions. I guess, we passed, because he continued.

"I don't have to tell you that those two pillars are established by God and have the magnetic strength and stability. The Sun is the closest source of Light and the rough ashlar Stone provides us with stability." – Albert Pike informed us with the confidence of a secret keeper. – "We are talking about the internal Magnet of Paracelsus. The grand magical agent is the AZOTH, the universal magnetic force. The Sun's Magnetic Force holds the Magnetic North of the Earth's geo-dynamo. That is why Horus, Moses and even Jesus held the Iron Rod of the Earth in high esteem. The Light of Life, our mental force and intellectual energy is derived from this Divine Magnetic Fire." – Pike instructed our seeker's mind.

"Brother Pike, can I ask a question." – I shouted the question toward the Illustrious Master. He nodded in agreement.

"Both you and I are Freemasons, Judeo-Christians and the carriers of the Peace Pipe of the Native Americans. Do you see the 'Channunpa' Peace Pipe as the symbolism for the Geo-dynamo of the Earth, Sir?" – I rattled off my question to Albert Pike.

"I let your adopted Father Medicine Man Francis Two Charger answer that question." - echoed the words of Pike as he disappeared in the mystic red clouds of the magicians.

"Daughter and Son, Hihanni Washte, Good Morning on this special day." – we heard Dad Two Charger greet us as he appeared on the scene.

"Hihanni Washte, Good Morning Dad." – we answered back enthusiastically.

He was dressed just in regular clothing and other than the Native American features, the dark hair and ponytail, he did not appear in full regalia.

"Son, did you get my message from that medium in Wisconsin?" – he was curious. 'So, it was real'- I thought to myself. Now, I remembered, … that as I was in the hospital, there came in a nice lady who had Pneumonia. As the hospital doctor I properly prepared to admit her and to start treatment. The nurses asked me if I knew who she was. I didn't. One of them informed me that she was a 'seer', a medium who number of people visited to get words from their deceased relatives. She even wrote a book. It was good to know, but so many of the fake medium we met in our lives that I was a little hesitant to believe in her authenticity initially. Anyway, I was not interested to talk to any of my dead relatives, I needed to get her into the hospital, ask her about her past medical history, allergies, so I can treat her correctly. Suddenly, as we were visiting about her medical issues, she closed her eyes and seemingly went into a trance. Moments later she opened her eyes and asked me if my father has already passed. I answered 'yes'. I was thinking of my biological father. She informed me that two elderly males appeared in her vision. The one up front was holding a pipe in his hands. Then the medium asked me.

"Was you grandfather and father collectors of pipes?" – the medium asked me.

"No, I don't think so." – I answered thinking of my biological grandfather Andras and my father Janos.

"Well, there are two males here, the one standing upfront is holding a pipe in his hands and suggesting to me that you have to take care of the pipe." – she insisted. "It is probably like some collector's item kept in your family." – the medium suggested. That is when the magical coin dropped that jolted my brain to remember. Wow! It was my Sioux Lakota adopted father, we called Dad Two Charger who appeared to her as my father and behind him was standing my real biological father. I assume, that Dad Two Charger wanted me to register that I need to 'take care of my pipe' and pray with it. Tears swollen up into a little river in my eyes and I had to leave the patient's room before I would start bawling. My colleagues, the doctors, nurses, and the staff did not know about my affiliation with our Sioux Lakota Indian family, thus the whole event the medium created felt very authentic. She was a real medium.

"Yes, Dad – You told her to tell me to take care of my pipe." – I answered my adopted father.

"Washte, that's right son." Dad Two Charger answered me back. I last seen him when Mom Two Charger passed, and I was one of the pallbearers on the Rosebud Reservation in South Dakota.

"Let me tell both of you about the 'Chan-nunpa' pipe of your Lakota ancestors. ... As you know 'Chan' means 'Wood' in our Lakota language." – he looked at us for reassurance. Eva and I both nodded. "Then you also know that 'Nunpa' means 'Two', since your given Indian name and my name 'Two Charger' is written as 'Nunpa Wacua'. 'Nunpa' meaning 'Two'. So, the pipe is called 'Wood Two', or in English word sequence "TWO WOOD". Do you remember that teaching?" – Dad Two Charger asked.

"We do." – both of us reassured our father.

"Then you both understand that the red stone of the pipe represents Mother Earth with its burning Core in the middle. Then, although we have only one stem coming out of the red stone pipe, we call it TWO WOOD, so you can understand that the Earth has TWO trees or two pillars that can shut down heaven, ... when we light the CHANNUNPA, the Sacred Pipe - the two AXES of the Earth unite into one stem and the smoke and fire coming out of the red stone reminds us the Day of Recreation that you came to learn about." – Dad explained.

"Yes." – I acknowledged the wisdom.

"The White Buffalo Maiden brought us this sacred pipe." – the simple medicine man informed us. This was the moment when the All-knowing Spirit brought into my feeble mind that maybe the White Buffalo Maiden is the astronomical equivalent of the Golden Calf of the Jewish Wisdom. If we could all stay astronomical in our creation mythologies than we would recognize the interrelatedness of the cosmic story.

"I can't believe the honor that we could be part of this discussion." – now Eva got soft on me.

"Eva, Star Woman, you are a 'heyoka' a 'joker, backwards walking medicine woman' of the best kind. You will teach this sacred knowledge to a lot of your extended family and friends for a long time to come. This is one of our gifts to the world from the ancient Lakota Sicangu 'Burnt Thigh' people." – Dad Two Charger addressed my wife. – "As the White Buffalo Calf Maiden came to the Lakota Tribe to bring the Sacred Pipe, the same way you two will spread the wisdom of the Chante Luta, the Red Heart of the Sacred Buffalo. Now, you start understanding that this cosmic event we are referring to on March 26th, the Day of Re-Creation came many moons ago, but we maintained the HEART OF THE BUFFALO, just as you maintained the HEART OF THE TAURUS BULL, that is the PLEIADES, the HEART OF

THE GOLDEN ELK – 'chante hehaka' (heart of elk)." – Dad Two Charger connected the wisdom.

"Wow, … that is why we placed an actual Buffalo Heart under the Sundance Tree where the roots would be?!" – Eva burst out with this new epiphany. Our medicine man Dad smiled at his daughter. My wife proudly exclaimed. "I start understanding the cosmic meanings." – Eva baldly proclaimed.

"Every ceremony we taught you two have deep cosmic meanings. Cherish it daughter chunkshi!" – he said. "…and remember which was the forbidden direction during the Sundance you both participated in?" – Dad Two Charger looked at us mysteriously.

"The East." – we blurted out simultaneously.

"The East is where the Red Cloud comes at Christmas, and the EAST at EASTER is a sacred direction from where the black hole eruption comes from by the way of PLEIADES, the Heart of the Buffalo." – Dad Two Charger had a gentle smile. "That is why the east was the forbidden direction."

"What about the symbolism of the sacred Sweat Lodge then?" – my wife asked.

"I am glad you asked." – Dad raised his arms in front of his chest and made a circle with his two palms flattening his thumbs on the bottom. He took a deep breath before he began his explanation.

"The sweat lodge is a half-circle above ground. In the middle pit we place heated volcanic rocks. We pour the water on those hot volcanic rocks to show how the geo-dynamo works with the core inside the Earth. We make it hot to remind the praying members of the Oyate (='people'), how hot will it get when the Earth's axes shift. … This is the same teaching of Jesus Christ walking in the desert heat for 40 days." – Dad Two Charger explained with passion. "Mom, Shte, James are all here with us and sending their love. Tell that to the rest of the family. Remember your people, your family in these changing times." – Dad Two Charger suddenly disappeared in a Red Cloud as a reminder of the Prophecy. Four medicine men reappeared dressed in the colors of the four directions. They waived comically to us as it was a theatrical production. Dad was holding up the arm of Chief Leonard Crow Dog, who just passed on 6/6/21 and was not expected to be out here so soon. The other two of the four medicine men we could not recognize as they faded into the Cloud, but we had the feeling that they will reappear soon to teach us some cosmic wisdom – as they tried when they were alive. Crow Dog turned back and faced us like 'ask me'.

"Grandpa Crow Dog. You are from the Sicangu 'Burnt Thigh' Oyate Nation of the Rosebud Reservation. Thank You for fighting for the Religious Freedom of all the tribes. If it was not your persistence, with all the other members of your organization, Russell and John and the others, we would not learn about the incredible cosmic wisdom your people implanted in the sacred ceremonies. Mitakuye Oyasin, we are all related." – I offered my thanks to this great spiritual warrior.

"Mitakuye Oyasin, we are all related." – smiled Leonard Crow Dog in our direction before fading into the Red Cloud after the others. We were about to focus back on Thoth's direction, but unexpectedly another medicine man stepped out of the Red Cloud.

"Just so you know this, our sacred and secret creation legends say that it will be the emergence of the Red Cloud that will begin our New Dawn soon." – said Chief Waukon Decorah, the leader of the Ho-chunk Indian tribe 200 years ago. We both were blown away that this chief would appear to us. We live on a small island today in Wisconsin surrounded by a river that comes out of the Decorah Lake we look at daily, that received its name from this tribal leader. His headdress was interesting as four palm sized pillars emerged on top. He was a hand some fellow and his appearance gave a special meaning to the place we are currently residing on.

"Red Cloud, we'll remember." – Eva greeted him.

"So many paths we have taken and so many great teachers we met on this sacred path." – I looked at my wife to see if she was as touched by the visit of great tribal chiefs, deceased family members and great legendary teachers.

"I wouldn't mind talking to Mom Two Charger at one point on our journey." – she sighed.

"I am here daughter, chunkshi." – Mom Two Charger appeared to us. "You are talking about Red Cloud, Flying Hawk, Spotted Tail of the Deer, Spotted Elk, Black Elk. These are warriors, who maintained the cosmic knowledge for their people. Our tribe was placed on the Reservation and our knowledge suppressed. We could not pray our own way until 1973. We secretly maintained the important knowledge through oral traditions in our names, in our ceremonies without even having paper to write down thousands of years of wisdom. The 'washichu' took almost everything from us. … Okay, chunkshi let us talk about our family history that you were adopted into in 1994, then your children Rubina and Austin in 1995. Your Dad, Francis Two Charger received his name from Two Charger, who was the younger son of Two Strikes. Two Strikes is your great grandpa. We live in the town named after him. There are archive pictures from the late 1800's where they show Two Strikes being one of the Lakota chiefs who negotiated with the American Government in the Congress in Washington, DC for our lands. Two Strikes' mother was one of the female relatives of Sitting Bull, another great Lakota Chief. Sitting Bull was the uncle of Flying Hawk, who was the cousin of Crazy Horse. Flying Hawk participated in Red Cloud's War of 1866-1868 and all other major wars. You see chunkshi we name our brave chiefs after main cosmic events, so we can remember. Chief Red Cloud was there at most famous battles, and he was there when Crazy Horse died. His Mother was Iron Cedar Woman. These are all names that refer to cosmic secrets that we could have brought to the white race whose leaders hide the truth from their own people. All these names and our ceremonies have cosmic significance, but our knowledge was wiped from the tribe and now we are trying to bring it back from the other side. You have to share it back with your tribe." – explained Mom Marie Two Charger, the daughter of Kills Plenty. "Your Dad got his medicine bundle from the famous medicine man Picket Pin.

That is the medicine our family continues to carry, that is what the two of you part of. Stay on the Chanku Luta - Red Road and our family names and sacred ceremonies will be honored and help you understand what is to come. A lot of us are rooting for you. There are not many of you, seekers comfortable sitting in a pew of the church and synagogue or on the sweat lodge floor with Dad." – Mom Two Charger disappeared in the Red Cloud behind her without much fanfare.

"Your Mom must love you a lot." – Thoth reappeared on the Golden Throne of the Temple. The THRONE had its own astronomical secret. It was the 'W' shaped Cassiopeia who gave the idea for the Throne. Knowing that either side of the ZERO Hour housed the Queen and the King.

"They both do. Both moms, loved me a lot. My biological Mom's last name is Elk. So, knowing that sacred connection to the Day of Re-Creation from both mothers, I was able to learn from - is an honor I never forget. I thank the Holy Spirit, Adonai, Jesus, the Almighty Living God, Great Spirit for all these gifts." - my wife said with overwhelming joy in her voice.

4.

Know Your Science

Thoth crossed his arms in front of his chest adoring the mention of the One Living God. - "We need to get back to the hard science of the Universe. Your time is limited. If you fail, we failed you and took you from Earth into the Dreamtime. That will affect too many others. So, let us learn about the rhythm of our Galaxy that runs through our body. Our heartbeat, and the heartbeat of Mother Earth. This is the Rhythm that comes from the Mouth of God from the Center of the Universe. It is the 'WORD', it is what everything is made of." - Thoth stated. "Let me show you an example of the rhythm. Starting from the Center of the Universe there is only one rhythm, one verse that comes out of the Mouth of God. It is the only song that resonate out from the center and allows creation to happen from that. Like dropping a pebble into the center of a lake, which would represent the Universe, the living water creates concentric circles, ripples that go out toward the edges and constantly create galaxies and solar systems full of life. It is the 4+1=5 or even the 5+5=6 unified rhythm of the creating Universe."

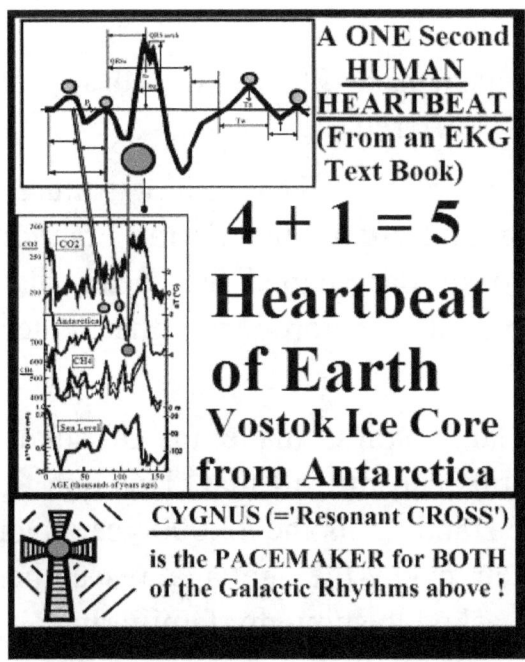

A ONE Second **HUMAN HEARTBEAT** (From an EKG Text Book)

4 + 1 = 5

Heartbeat of Earth

Vostok Ice Core from Antarctica

CYGNUS (='Resonant CROSS') is the PACEMAKER for BOTH of the Galactic Rhythms above !

"Here is a very good example. The 1 SECOND heartbeat of a Human has the 4 + 1 = 5 style

Cosmic Rhythm. As above so below. Then the 115,720 years long Ice Age rhythm, similarly, has the SAME 4 + 1 = 5 heartbeat rhythm for our Earth's geo-dynamo. Then each finger of the ICE AGE 4 + 1 HAND is about 23,144 years long. There are 5 fingers each last 23,114 years, thus 5 x 23,144 = 115,720 years. Each finger is divided into four parts of 5,786 years." - Thoth paused. "A full Ice Age is 20 x 5,786 years, that is 115,720 years." – Thoth paused to see if we understand his numbers.

The Mayans used 20 as the basis of their calendar." – I offered.

"Exactly, 4 x 5 is 20. That is how Nature works. … Do you understand the Spiral Fractions that create these similar shaped heartbeats that come out of the Spiral Pair Force from the Center of the Universe?"

"Only a large spiral made up of smaller and smaller spirals can full fill that. This one finger of the Cosmic Hand, … is the 23,000 years Dominant Milankovitch cycle the ice age researchers talk about?" – I asked to show my familiarity.

"Yes. The 23,000 years long finger is the dominant rhythm if you talk about one finger of God. The 4 + 1 = 5 rhythm symbolizes the Hand of God, that is the 'Hamsa', the Five. … Okay, getting back to the exact 23,144 years long dominant finger – it has 4 divisions, each 5,786 years. 23,144 / 4 = 5,786." – He looked up and stuck his pointing finger up for us to see and slowly turned it around in all four directions. "ONE direction of a Finger of God is about 5,786 years long, North, East, South and West – then the temperature of Earth changes again with every direction." – He turned his finger another 90 degrees as he was explaining. It is very simple." – a shadow of an almost imperceptible smile ran through his face. Eva and I looked at each other and twirled our fingers as good students would do.

"Okay, you remember that the Mayan Calendar counting is based on the number 20. That is how many toes and fingers we have on our extremities thus it makes sense. God also creates in 20. During a 115,720 years long full ice age, the temperatures suddenly change directions 20 times. Then 20 x 5,786 = 115,720 years. The shortest time-period is then 5,786 years. Now, you will have to figure out what are the cosmic factors, which shift the temperature every 5,786 years. ... Am I going too fast?" – Thoth smiled. He looked to the side to notice a well-dressed middle-aged male walk into the scene.

The Egyptian palace had two large columns to Thoth's right that were round as the stalk of the reed or water lily they represented. At the top they widened out into the flower with petals. We understood that these represented the Milky Way River where these cosmic reeds would grow. The slightly faded red, yellow, and green colors made the tall and thick columns authentic. The gilded boxes and the life size lion, ram, goat, and bull statues tastefully decorated the background. A large gold emblem of the Winged Disk was placed above the large entrance gate on the East. It was a reminder of the Destroyer of Humanity. The man who walked in between the two reed pillars stopped there in the cross line. His dark gray 3 pieces suit was old-style, but charmingly elegant. The black tie fit him well. Coming from the era of Albert Einstein about a 100 years ago, this well-situated Serbian gentleman was a respectable looking scientist from the Austro-Hungarian Empire. He lived in Budapest until the beginning of the First World War. Budapest is very dear to my heart since that is where I grew up between the ages of 5 until 22.

"I do not like to just walk in on any conversations, but this is very dear to my heart." – Milutin Milankovitch, the legendary Serbian scientist stated. "Since I was the one who developed the scientific principles around my Milankovitch Theory therefore, I felt compelled to join this important discussion." – the Serbian mathematician stated with quiet confidence. "I am observing with pleasure from this Heavenly place that my original work is the accepted theory of the cycles of the ice ages. It feels me with satisfaction that what I wrote down over 100 years ago - now is being taught by NASA, NOAA, ESA, and others throughout the world." – Milankovitch introduced himself to us.

"How were you able to calculate it with such an accuracy?" – I asked the legendary mathematician.

"Willy, think of these two reed pillars as the two axes of the Earth." – Milutin reached out with his arms toward the pillars. "These pillars control the geo-dynamo and the cycles of the Earth."

"We are listening, professor." – I offered.

"You know that nowadays the Polar Axis is in 23.4 degrees angle from the Magnetic North. 'Thousands of years ago it was only 22.1 degrees. I calculated the Axial Precession, otherwise called the WOBBLE. I arrived to demonstrate the dominant cycle of the 23,000 years. Then I calculated out the axial tilt or OBLIQUITY, which turned out to be 41,000 years. The difference between the two is 41,000 – 23,000 = 18,000 years. That gave me another cycle. The variations in ECCENTRICITY provided the over 100,000 year long Full Ice Age cycle. Now, there was an 11,500years cycle that was half of the 23,000 years. The smallest cycle was about 5,750 years - quarter cycle. These are rounded numbers only." – Milutin stated with confidence.

"Apparently you were very close to the actual numbers, because the Russian – French ice core researchers of the Vostok (= 'EAST') project proved that you were right Sir. The 23,000years cycle maybe 23,144years long, but very accurate." – I assured the proud Serbian scientist.

"Willy, I was watching you from above proudly acknowledging that you wrote your first book, The Celestial Clock – in which you tried to educate the public about these recurrent cycles. Do you feel now that it was worth it, ... that you reached enough people with this important message?" – Milutin Milankovitch asked me. I shook my head sideways.

"When over 20 years ago you discovered that the 115,720years long Milankovitch Ice Age rhythm morphologically resembled the one second human heartbeat ... I was very proud of you. When you were invited to talk about it on the Art Bell Show on February 10th, 2001 – I was sure that you will get noticed. Years after that when Giorgio interviewed you for the Ancient Aliens, I was sure you will get some traction. They did not even air it.

You know that they are not true scientist. But when you gave your ice age graph and the heartbeat graph to the amazing Dr. Ben Carson the world-famous doctor in 2016, I was sure that you and I will make some headlines. It did not happen." – Milankovitch sighed with some hint of sadness in his voice.

"I tried." – I stated. "… So, what is amazing here that we can see that the ONE SECOND HUMAN HEARTBEAT morphologically equals the 115,720 years long ONE ICE AGE CYCLE – an important cosmic fact and nobody cares." – I sighed again.

"How many heartbeats in a year?" – Eva cut in entertaining her own curiosity.

"31 million 557, 600." – Milutin Milankovitch answered quick before I even could begin my own calculations.

"So, a One second heartbeat of a human equals to the Ice Age Heartbeat of the Earth. That would be the ultimate 'as above so below' example." – Eva echoed. " … the two heartbeats Earth's and the human are hundreds of trillions of times more in magnitude, but still the same configuration, 4 + 1. So, imagining that there are millions of different types of lives, including aliens out there in the Universe who look like us, does not seem too strange after all." – Eva concluded. Mr. Milutin Milankovitch sounded off a few claps above his head with his outstretched arms and he began to walk out on the East Gate.

"Sir, may I ask one more question?" – I shouted toward the scientist. He stopped and turned around.

"Certainly, you may. That is why I showed up for you." – He looked at me politely.

"In this 'prophet school' here - I am learning that those ice age cycles that you have identified are now seemed to be switched from cold to warm and warm to cold by the two most important black hole eruptions, the Orion Nebula and the Cygnus Swan. That is now my Gaspar Theory - building on your Milankovitch Theory. How should I handle that?" – I looked at the amazing scientist. "Can I use your name and studies to tie to my astronomical research and connect the two?" – I asked Milankovitch.

"Okay Willy, you have my permission to call 'our' theory the **Gaspar-Milankovitch Theory of Recurring Ice Ages**. Your friend John Major Jenkins already name you that in his book titled Galactic Alignment. So, this is just a formality, but an important one. Thank You for asking for my permission, … you don't need it, but it felt good.

120

Honor needs to run this world." – Milankovitch bowed to us in respect and slowly walked out.

"Now, this is powerful you must admit." – Thoth exclaimed proudly. "Your name will be paired to the Milankovitch name in scientific circles. People will finally know that the smallest electrical force that moves the human heartbeat every second is the same exact shape and rhythm that moves the huge Earth. So, my conclusion is that whatever electro-magnetic power comes out of the Center of the Universe, comes out of our Galaxy, our Sun and our Earth" - Thoth seemed very confident in what he was saying.

"Look at the picture. It may not be the most scientifically constructed, but I try to keep it simple to be effective. On this graph I projected to the wall here, you will see the largest dynamo from the Center of the Universe moves like the Earth dynamo. Down to the smallest white dwarf stars. Down to the smallest subatomic particles. But that is not in the news, yet." – Thoth claimed.

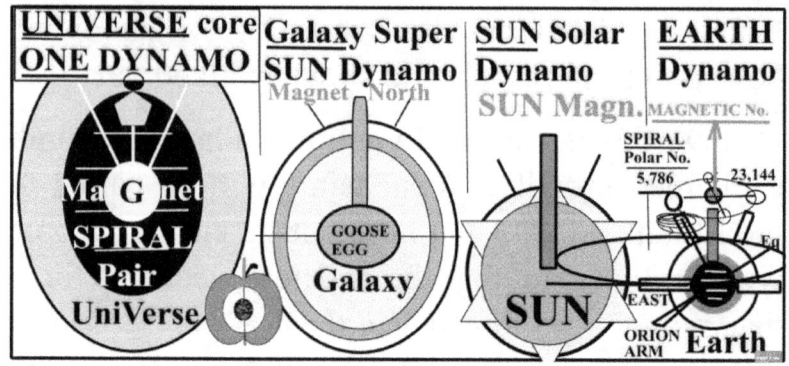

"So, if the Earth's geo-dynamo has its TWO POLES, the Magnetic North, and the Polar North, then it is the same for the Sun's Solar Dynamo, the Galactic Dynamo, the Universal Dynamo of God. All work on the same electro-magnetic principles. It is simplified, but it is the only way, as above so below works. When you have the Earth's geo-dynamo energetic system, it recharges every about 5,800 years. That is what you're learning from us." – said Thoth

"So, the Red Cloud Prophecy says that the end of this year or next year around Christmas the Orion Nebula will erupt and produce a nice Red Cloud or Red star. That is the beginning?" – I asked Thoth.

"Why would it happen now and not in another year or a hundred years? Are we due for a scheduled recharge of our Earthly geo-dynamo?" – Eva was right on with her question.

"Okay, as you both know the climate period lasts about 5,786 years. The Jewish Year is 5,781 this year in the first half of 2021 and turns to 5,782 after September 2021. Therefore, 5,786 – 5,782 = 4 years. That would give us 4 more years after the end of this year. But the 5,786 years cycle ends with the 4th year of the countdown. **That gives the beginning of the last 14 years as 25th December 2021/2022. The actual year of the RECHARGE is 2026. That is the year of the AXIS SHIFT."** – Thoth reassured us. "But, having said that – only Father God knows this and nobody else. Not even me. I am also guessing based on the previous historical instances." – Thoth admitted.

"What else would say that we are entering the last 14 years now?" – Cutie asked. "There had to be a more exact way of foretelling it." – She was hoping to avoid these calamities. Thoth nodded.

"There are several pieces of information for that. Some of it I will not tell you, because it will be on your exam, and you need to figure that out or you will not be the prophets we hoped you would." – Thoth Hermes exclaimed.

"Where is some proof that the Ancients knew about this time frame?" – I asked.

"Let us talk about generations." – Thoth said. "How many male warriors and female wives were in your ancient Magyar creation legend? I mean the two brothers, Hunor (Perseus) and Magor (Orion – connected to the Magnetic North) who were the first two sons of the Great Hunter NIMROD. We know that the founding father of the Hungarian Magyar nation was Nimrod, who is Orion. That is where the closest black hole to Earth is located, so the legend is a cosmic secret and not a true human story. Just like all the others around the world." – Thoth smiled.

"So, to answer your question Hermes, there were TWO BROTHERS and 50 warriors who went to hunt for the Golden Elk. That is 52 males. They met TWO PRINCESSES who had 50 handmaids. That is 52 females. They all got married to each other and these 104 people started the Hungarian Magyar nation. Is that a good start for a generation?" – I asked the great Thoth Mercury Hermes Trismegistus.

"It takes 52 years for the MALE Sun King to meet up with the FEMALE Moon Princess in the same place in the sky. So, a generation is defined as 52 years. It is very important!" – Thoth emphasized.

"So, if I use 110 generations - as I read it in the Kolbrin Bible – then 110 x 52 = 5,720. Using the

124

Hebrew Calendar that would be 1960. Nothing happened in 1960. Okay, maybe Elvis and the Beatles." – I was contemplating and joking around.

"Some secret societies would use the 52 generations x 111.0 or 111.1. The 111 would take you to the Hebrew Year of 5,772 that was in the year of the Mayan Calendar Ending 2012. 111.1 generations would take you to 2017. Certainly, you can start with 5,786 and divide it by 52 and you will get 111.269 generations. Furthermore, you can take the 5,786 and divide it with the Kolbrin generations of 110, which then gives you 52.6 generations." – Thoth looked up.

"But none of these are the ultimate numbers, right? So, what is the Big Secret about this?" – Eva jumped into the conversation.

"The Great Pyramid of Giza is built to have an angle of 51.50. You either have think that those awesome scientists missed the angle by a half a degree and were too sloppy building that colossal structure for us to solve … or as superb cosmic scientists they built in another number that no one can forget. … I vote for the latter." – Thoth stated it triumphantly. He stared at us with a questioning face.

"Okay, let's go backwards then to see that number." – I ventured. – "5,786 divided by 51.50, right? It is roughly 112.35 generations. I can do it like 112.35 x 51.50 = 5,786, that is 2026, right?" – I was calculating with fever.

"You got it!" – Thoth screamed out loud. This was the first time we seen him being so animated and excited. "This is the most exciting cosmic science! None of our students so far solved this question."

"Wow. I was just counting backwards." – I looked up with surprise.

"Now, if you can tell me what is so amazing about the 112.35 generations, what is that number based on, … why the amazing builders had to change the design of the angle of the pyramid from 52 to 51.50 degrees … then I will be amazed by the both of you and as far I am concerned, you became a prophet. You do not have to take any more test." – Thoth eyes were twinkling. "I let you and Eva figure this out while I sit back." – the Stork leaned back on his golden throne.

"Okay, let's take the 110 out and we are left with 2.35. In numerology, 2 plus 3 is 5 and if we add, another five is 10. That is the perfect 10." – Eva went through some quick thinking.

"Good thinking, but it is not what I am looking for." – Thoth stated it. "The answer has to be based on the ultimate scientific base of the Universe, the creative force." – Thoth was radiant.

"Well, $1 + 1 + 2 + 3 + 5 = 12$" – I offered.

"Pretty good, but it is much bigger than that." – Thoth concluded.

"Okay, Cutie let's figure it out." – I offered to my wife.

"Alright, … we need to look at the exact definition of what Thoth tells us." – Eva talked like Thoth was not even there. We were going to solve this.

"He said to use the idea of the creative force, that is the scientific base of the Universe." – I recalled. Thoth let out a bird calling. We ignored it. We were on the path of discovery.

"What, the electro-magnetism?" – Eva asked.

"The spirit?" – I wondered.

"What was the base for the heartbeat of the Earth and the heartbeat of the Ice Age cycle?" – Eva wondered. - "Whatever generates those heartbeats is the answer."

"Let me help out a little bit." – Thoth butt in likely feeling ignored by us.

"We would appreciate that." – I answered.

"Okay, let's say the generation is not only 112.35, but 112.35813. Even better. 0-1-1-2-3-5-8-13-21, etc. ... Does that help?" – Thoth was grinning with enjoyment.

"Wait, those are the FIBONACCI NUMBER SEQUENCE!" – Eva was screaming it out loud.

"That's it. The Fibonacci Sequence." – I shouted.

"That is the base of the SPIRAL. We live in a SPIRAL GALAXY and a SPIRAL UNIVERSE." – Eva was excited beyond belief.

"The pyramid is like a Christmas Tree. Very much like a spiral shape increasing from top down." – I said.

"So, millions of people worked on building the Great Pyramid of Giza, which hid the amazing number that ends the cycle." – Eva concluded.

"51.50 x 112.35 = 5,786.025 ... or

"51.50 x 112.3581321 = 5,786.4438, so even when we go out further on the Fibonacci Number Sequence, we are still getting the Hebrew Year 5786, which is the year 2026. That's amazing" – I stated it with joy. This was a huge discovery Thoth shared with us.

51.5x112.35=5,786

"The Secret of the SPIRAL Fibonacci Number Sequence in the construction of the Great Pyramid." – I looked at Eva and we both turned to Thoth.

"Thank You Thoth, this Eternal Wisdom will stay with us forever." – Eva realized the gift.

"So, this year 2026 is very important mile marker in the climate shift, but the sequence of events starts December 25th, 2021?" – I asked this time trying to get all the help we will need for our finals, although it seemed like we will not take it after all. "You have to admit that it's a lot of new material that will take time to sink in. I want to make it back home in one piece. … It does not hurt to ask." – I was pleading.

"Okay. Let us go through the sequences of events from the past and the mythologies that support that." – Hermes Trismegistus suggested it.

"Okay, how do we know that the last time it happened was on December 25?" - I asked.

"We understand it by knowing the exact star constellations, the Astronomy of the Day of

December 24th – 25th among the Eastern sky." – Thoth said it as succinct as he could.

Suddenly, an extreme bright light filled the palace. It was so bright we had to squint with our eyes. It became a little less bright and we were able to look. A DARK SHADOW walked in.

"I am here to confirm." – we looked over to see who walked into this beautiful Egyptian Temple. It was the pre-dynastic Scorpion King. "I, the Scorpion King with the famous sting of the scorpion started the first 3 years, the 4th one is already the Re-Creation."

We were still paralyzed from the sudden marching in of the Scorpion King. He noticed that we were stunned, and he posed for a few seconds to allow us time to refocus.

"Okay, there is roughly 33 years that happens between 2001 and 2034. That is a lifetime of Jesus Christ and Alexander the Great, who was also thought to be the Son of God by some. The dilemma is that different cultures registered the divisions of these years that separated the ages. The ancient cosmic story was always told in the present tense, but it truly pointed to the past when great events happened.

"Yes, not just the life of Christ and Alexander the Great, but even the Egyptian Dynasties are about the last 33 years of the roughly 5,800 years. Most importantly though, I – the Scorpion King start the last 14 years. The counting is confusing, but you can get it." – the Scorpion King assured us. "Actually, you better get it for your final exam. Or you're both dead." – He had an evil grin. Maybe it was a good smile but coming off the face of a Scorpion seemed negative.

4.

The International Day of December 25

The Scorpion King was an interesting looking human pharaoh walking upright in all black with his body curved. It did give him the air of being a scorpion, but he did not have the poisonous tail of the scorpion. He sported a scorpion emblem on the front of his White Crown for identification, I guess. He looked like a pharaoh with the White Crown hat.

"This is how they know me. The king, not the pharaoh." – the Scorpion King announced. "Predynasty. I was the first king. The dynasty began with the 4th year of the last 14 years and that is when the pharaohs appeared. Cute, hah?"

"How do we know that you are connected to the Eastern sky of December 24th, don't you have to be Jesus Christ, Krishna or Mithra?" – I asked.

"Show them the star credentials." – Thoth Hermes Trismegistus called on the Scorpion King.

"I have a few pictures from the Venus Temple of the Dendera Zodiac." – the Scorpion King stated.

"This is the picture from the Venus Temple in Egypt that shows me, the SCORPION KING on the East direction on December 25th. This is star knowledge, pure Astronomy and Cosmology." – the Scorpion King proudly announced.

Eva and I looked at each other like, this not a joke, there is the Scorpion below the Hawk that represents the Magnetic North that is secretly connected to the Orion Nebula black hole. So, the Scorpion is really in the creation mythologies.

"Okay, I could not wait." – Ya-Hoe, the famous Chinese Emperor walked into the room. He passed by the Scorpion King, but only looked at him from the corner of his eyes. His elaborate custom and crown that had little pompons hanging off the side, reminded me some over decorated French tapestry.

"I already said this to my Chinese seers." – he said.

I looked at Eva to see if she was as lost as I was. She made a funny face at me then turned to the emperor.

"What was that you said, oh Holly Emperor?" – she asked him in a slightly theatrical fashion.

"What I said exactly is – **that when a red star will appear in the sky coming out of the claw of the Scorpion in the eastern sky, then the end of an age is at hand.**" – the emperor raised his right hand without turning around and four strong China men appeared carrying a throne on two large logs. They lowered the throne for the emperor, who jumped in faster than expected. They lifted the throne with the chubby ruler inside, someone threw a small red smoke bomb and they evaporated into thin air.

We directed our attention back to the Scorpion.

"King Scorpion, - excuse the emperor for his interruption, but now looking at that picture you are showing us, why is there a female wolf … right behind you with bulging nipples ready to be milked?" – Eva asked.

The Scorpion King turned toward her, wanted to answer, but as soon as he opened his mouth - a couple of young toddlers walked by. One of them pointed to the Wolf mother and said proudly. – "Momma! Mama mia."

"Who are these toddlers?" – Eva broke out in a loud laugh pointing at the little ones who walked away waiving to the wolf. It was comical to see them wobble, and the Scorpion followed them out with his eyes.

"Romulus and Remus – the Twin Brothers who founded Rome" – the Scorpion King explained with a smile. "The Lupus Wolf Mother behind me on that picture is their mom who fed them from her tits."

"How did the Egyptians know who is going to establish the city of Rome?" – Eva asked again.

"They didn't. We had the strict and advanced astronomical and magical teachings in the Mystery School of Egypt known only to a select group of viziers. We gave them the idea for their own creation legend in their culture. Moses was one of the brightest viziers early on - being in the royal family of the Pharaoh. Alexander the Great also attended. The best student who became better than his teachers was Jesus Christ. He truly had a godly spark in him." – the King explained.

"Wait, you are only a made-up story about an astronomical marker from a celestial event, how did you pass on anything real to the Romans." – Eva laughed at the nonsensical situation.

"Exactly, … you're very smart." – the Scorpion King stated with ease as he made a funny grimace.

"Now, finally we agree on something." – Eva was laughing full-heartedly. "I see inconsistencies."

I looked over to her and made a face to slow her down a little bit. Then her face turned serious. "Can I ask you something more about that picture?" – Cutie was using a little bit more stern voice.

"That's why we are here." – the King agreed.

"Why do you and the pregnant hypo have those bubbles on your tails in the picture?" – my wife was curious. "It is pretty obvious, and it has to mean something very important."

"Excellent observation. I don't think that you are ready for the scientific explanation." – the Scorpion King looked around and set his glaze on the great Hermes Trismegistus, who graciously nodded that it was allowed to talk about the bubbles. - "It is difficult to talk about something that has not really made it to the scientific news and not in the consciousness of the population. You can read the Tulli Papirus." – The Scorpion King turned back to Thoth, who again nodded approvingly about the subject. – "You will see the Winged Disk there. …   Okay, … when the black hole erupts, the surrounding hydrocarbon gas bubbles from the atmosphere are pushed into Earth's climate. It is a huge gas bubble tsunami, like oil." – the Scorpion King mimicked with his hands eruptions.

"These multi-colored hydrocarbon bubbles can be spinning in the sky with high speed, and they usually carry extremely high temperatures." – the Scorpion looked up and it was obvious that he had a difficult time talking about the subject. "That is why the Egyptians called the Winged Disk - the

LORD. Yes, they called him the Lord! These are just almost like crude oil and gas spinning."

"Wow, that is … different." – I proclaimed, not founding a better expression for my surprise.

"That was the best example … to bring the idea of the poison of the tail of the scorpion into the climate picture." – the Scorpion stated. "Just as the poison of the scorpion sting brings heat and toxicity to the victim, this black hole eruption with the hydrocarbon gas bubbles did the same for the whole humanity in the past." - it was expressed with solemn sadness.

"How do we know that it came from the black hole?" – I asked.

"On the above picture, between the Wolf and myself, there is the Hawk with the White Crown on his head. As you know, the White Crown called 'Hedjet' on the top of the head of the Hawk is the representation of the shape of the Binary Black Hole. That Binary Black Hole from the Orion Nebula is what erupted." – the Scorpion stated.

"Wow!" – now my wife became surprised.

"Then if you look at the pregnant hippopotamus standing in front of me on that picture, she represents the energy built up in the ocean and she also has the tail made of bubbles. … She also has on her head the White Crown of the Binary black hole shape." – the Scorpion King was excited to be able to explain the science.

"Has anybody ever revealed anything to you this serious - about these cosmic secrets?" – the Scorpion King asked laughing confidently.

"Never!" – Eva and I looked at each other. "This is the first time we seen anything this deep scientifically. It is pretty repulsing."

"Those 'experts' who read these ancient pictures as Egyptologists - have no clue of what the picture displays scientifically. It is sad!" – the Scorpion stated. "Okay, here is another picture of me where I am a pharaoh, and my scorpion animal symbol of the star constellation is above me in the Eastern sky on Christmas. Then above the scorpion in the sky is the 'rosetta' light eruption from the black hole". – the Scorpion King proudly announced.

"Who could tell the science of a black hole eruption from that picture." – Eva remarked.

"Well, it is not easy for an average human to learn all these scientific facts from these fairy tale pictures. … You are now, in your present conditions are not humans." – the Scorpion informed us.

"Well, it seems almost impossible for us humans to accept this." – Eva stated it and I nodded in agreement.

BINARY Black Hole
Fans -Heat
Rosetta Eruption Scorpion
Compass Mer
Scorpion Macehead - Ashmolean Museum, Oxford

"The Ashmolean Museum in Oxford, England is an important place to keep valuable information. This Orion Nebula black hole eruption is the beginning of the last 14 years. If our calculations are right then this Christmas, December 25th, we will see again that firework. It has not happened in 5,786 years and almost nobody expects it. How easy it is for us etheric beings to read it and find the science in it, while you humans have no clue what these depictions mean." – the Scorpion King elaborated.

"Nobody can read this like you do." – I stated with a little flattery. "But if you teach us these secrets, we promise to share it with others." – I stated.

"You have no idea!" – the Scorpion smiled. "You will have to learn it, too. Sharing it is almost impossible until it happens." – he gazed at us.

A huge light filled the temple, and everything seemed to disappear for a few seconds and then we noted the most incredible human being standing in the middle of the room with a halo above His head.

"I had the cosmic teaching wrapped into the conception and the birth. So, my teaching about the Red Blazing Star of Bethlehem at my conception was also great allegorical cosmic teaching?" – Jesus Christ mysteriously appeared on the scene. "The Scorpion King story was an idea that did not appeal to regular people. Most folks don't like 'bugs', but it is a more truthful depiction of the actual cosmic science." – Christ stated with an innocent stare.

"My story was about God's love and the salvation of humanity, not some scorpion poison people could not relate to." – He floated across the marble floor with his sandals - inches above the ground. "Now, I wish we would have incorporated the Scorpion."

He was wearing a simple white toga, but still appeared majestic. Eva and I were in a state of incredible excitement seeing God in His human form. Christ started to talk to us again.

"The Red Cloud appeared at Christmas at my conception, … or birth, how ever you look at it. If I could just teach the truth to one priest or minister. Well, I have to go now, but I will be back." – He smiled gently. "I came Willy because you were thinking in your mind that I was much gentler and humane in my teachings. It is true, but you must learn the Scorpion tale." – He disappeared.

"Wow!" – I looked at Eva and was screaming with excitement. This was out of this world. "Jesus Christ, my Lord and Savior." – I repeated it with insane excitement several times to calm down my spirit. The Lord was gone before I noticed.

Suddenly, a great Catholic, who happened to be the descendant of the Last Mayan Kings appeared.

"Eva and Willy, I have two scorpion stories to share with you. Remember when we talked about the Popol Vuh? It was about the Mayan Creation legends. There was the Red Cloud at dawn on the eastern sky. Dr. Pepe Jaramillo, yourself and I tried to figure out what it meant. Remember? Also, we seen the Scorpion by the World Tree at the Mayan Creation, but we did not understand, yet" –

the voice came from the Mayan Don Gaspar Antonio Xiu. "We did not know yet that the Orion Nebula was a runaway black hole. The scientist kept it from us until 2012." – Don Gaspar explained.

"How did you get here mi hermano?" – I asked with surprise. He shrugged his royal shoulders. I could not help it. A sudden saccadic cry broke up out of me when I realized that this Mexican friend, who was the last surviving adult member of the Royal Mayan Xiu family was dead. The Last Mayan King. The history books tell us that it was the royal Mayan XIU family in 751 AD who established the Mayan city of Uxmal.

My great friend, Dr. Jose Jaramillo, who is a well-known Mayan scholar, introduced us during a Mayan Calendar 2012 Conference in San Diego in 2008. Don Gaspar, just as Pepe Jaramillo and myself were speakers there. It was the San Diego Conference on Maya Calendar 2012. Dr. Jaramillo was the organizer, and he was in my mind one of the best Mayan scholars still alive today. His grandma was half Mayan from the Yucatan and that gave him an impetus to dig deep into the Mayan mysteries.

"I still needed to learn so much from you Don Gaspar, just as I wanted to tell you about all the new discoveries we found." – I was still sobbing.

"Willy, my friend, I will be back during this etheric process to help you, Eva and Pepe to fully understand some of the mysteries that are just coming out. Up here we see everything at once. We understand everything in spirit. I could not explain to you, but we see ahead. You have nothing to worry about. You hang in there and I will see you both later - on this exciting journey. Do not cry, we live on this side, we don't have our senses, so we don't get hungry, we don't lust after things, we do not have pain, we don't hurt, but we do remember, talk without voices, visit and try to influence the ones living in the flesh." – the Mayan King assured me.

I nodded, but still did not hear everything he said.

"Remember, when Pepe, Eva and you went to visit the Chichen Itza pyramid with a Mexican group?" – Don Gaspar asked. I nodded with agreement and the remembering of the event stopped me from crying like an idiot. – "Remember that it was March 20th - and the hotel gave away your rooms, because you got there late and there were so many people, they needed those rooms?" – He looked at us with love and I nodded, still trying to get my composure. I sure remember that there were 30 – 50,000 visitors coming there to see the two serpent lights descending on the stair of the pyramid to celebrate the Re-Creation.

Most of them, almost all of them did not even understand the significance.

"Do you remember that you had to go into an old rundown motel, where a scorpion was living under the stone foundation of your bed?" – he was laughing.

"I remember. The darn thing did not want to leave. Eva and I gently chased it out, we settled on our bed when we noticed the Scorpion rushing back into the room under the gaping space of our door. His tail was raised to scare us, and it just moved into the crack under the bed. I grabbed my tennis shoes and was ready to smash the little 'bug', but Eva stopped me. 'Let him live'. So, I did." – I was able to smile about it now.

"I am glad you did not smash it. That was a Mayan Elder who visited the two of you that night." – Don Gaspar continued.

"That is unbelievable, … but you know Grandpa Don Gaspar I suspected that." – Eva shouted.

"While the two of you were sleeping soundly, he installed a dream into your minds about the Day of Conception at Christmas and the Day of Re-Creation, March 26th that the Chichen Itza pyramid builders wanted to encode in the building. Unfortunately, everybody already forgot the cosmic secrets. … But here we are!" – The Mayan King sounded theatrical.

I was about to ask him a question about the Descending God, the Bee Prince of Tulum, but he already faded out. As soon as he appeared a few minutes ago, he now already disappeared, and the Egyptian Scorpion King was back in the picture.

"Everybody wants to tell their scorpion stories. Suddenly, I am popular again. Yes, I am in the Maya Creation stories, too - under the World Tree. I am under the bull in the Mithra killing the Bull scenes in Rome." – The Scorpion King smiled happily. - "I will show you another Egyptian picture that shows the Astronomy of Christmas on the East." – the Egyptian Scorpion King exclaimed.

"The Wolf is there and that tells you two that it is Christmas 5,786 years ago." – the Scorpion King was happy to teach.

"How many scorpions' related stories we have … and how come the Sumerians, Egyptians, Mayans, Greeks, Romans and the Chinese all used the same astronomical markers to bring attention to the date of December 25th?" – my wife asked.

"In this picture, we might be at Christmas in 2022, after we already had the tsunami a few weeks ago. The frogs are present, and the Boat is ready to depart on the raging seas. Kind of like the classical Greek story of Odyssey. The Greeks were good students but did not know everything." – the king said.

"Okay, I show you an astronomy picture without the scorpion. It is the same December 25th. So, here on this next picture we again show the time before Christmas and Hannukah. You can see the Lupus Wolf who again represents the time around December 25th. We can tell the time from looking to the left edge of the picture where the Double-headed Ram is. In Astronomy we call that the Second or the Double Ram point, that is the date of the Zero point. That is where the daily 24 hours begins. The date of the meeting point of the Solar Plain and the Equator is then November 8 - 9, thus the Ram lasts until the 19th - since each person is 10 days long decan." – He looked up. - "Thus, we can count that every person is 10 days. That takes us to around the Christmas time." – the Scorpion explained.

"Why is there a Vulture at the edge of the Boat?" – Eva asked.

"Why is there even a boat?" – I chimed in.

"Vulture hovers around areas of death. The beginning of the last 14 years forbode death. This seen is at the end of 2022 and the big tsunami already happened at the end of September. Death is in the air. Then the boat signifies that the Journey on the disturbed seas began. Kind of like the story of Odyssey." – the King proclaimed. It was easy to understand these pictures scientifically when he explained it, but how come none of us average humans could understand it. 'Black hole eruptions, scorpion tails, heated spinning hydrocarbon bubbles in the sky, binary black hole shaped white crowns on the pharaoh's head, … pretty weird stuff' – I was thinking to myself. The Scorpion King faded away and Thoth reappeared to us again.

"Ask specific questions that is about Cosmology." – Thoth asked us. He did not offer extra information. Eva was looking over to me to see if I can pick up the conversation a little better.

"We are here to learn from you I assume." – I hesitated. He nodded approvingly. – "Can I ask you big favor?" – I was begging Thoth. He graciously nodded again. His big thin beak looked a little strange on his thin head, but I accepted it as reality.

"If you will not understand the basics of the Cosmos, the Milky Way, the Sun, the Solar System, along with how the geo-dynamo is allowed to operate in this perfect system – you will never understand the creation mythologies. If you do not understand the science of this system, you will make up false stories about the animal symbols of Astronomy, such as the Bear is Russia, the Dragon is China, … and all that non-sense that is human stupidity." – Thoth was not kind to the biblical false prophets. "Look at this picture. The Dragon is between Polaris and Vega on 9-11!"

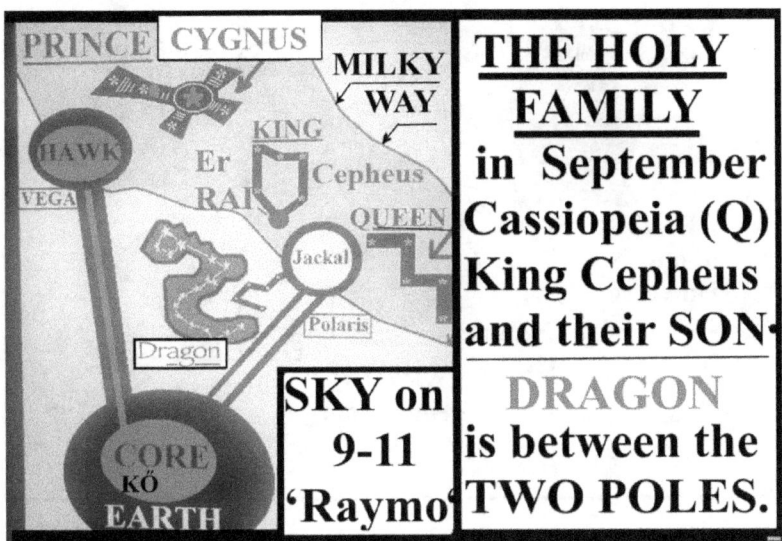

"The Coptic Christian New Year." – Thoth stated.

"You have to place the two axes of the Earth's geo-dynamo into the Milky Way Galactic model to start understanding the whole picture.

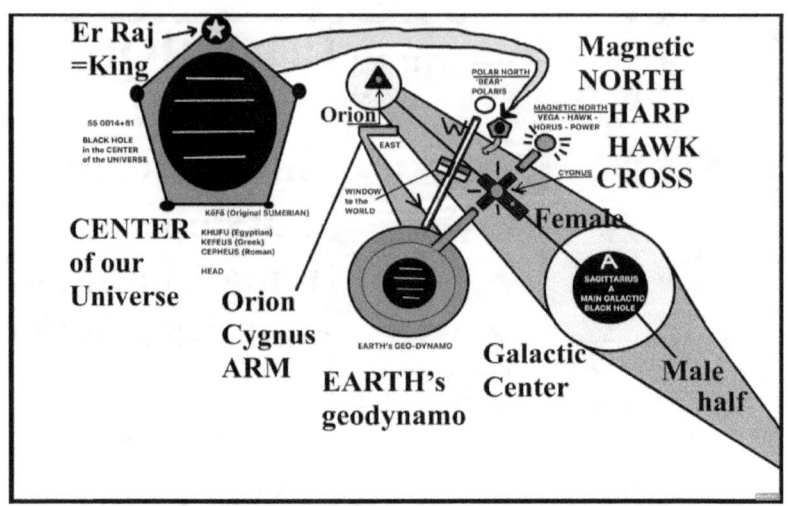

"That is very similar to what Santa showed us. Is this the template we need to memorize?" – I enquired. Thoth was studying my facial expression. Finally, he raised his head and began to talk.

"There is one major scientific fact that allows life to exist on our planet, other than the presence of water and oxygen. The mysterious Earth's geo-dynamo has been the force that allows life on Earth. It creates a magnetic shield against destructive UV light. It protects life on Earth for millions of years. That you need to know." – Hermes explained.

"Let us get familiar with the dynamo. I will teach you how the ancient Egyptians depicted the knowledge hidden behind animal deities that are related to the function of our globe." - Thoth said. "Let us learn the function of the geo-dynamo."

POLARIS **Polar North**   MAGNETIC NORTH **Magnetic NORTH**

VEGA Star in the HARP constellation Swooping Hawk HORUS / hERO IRON ROD of MOSES and also JESUS CHRIST! The Secret of the IRON ROD !!!! As taught by Thoth, Horus / ERO Moses, David, and Jesus Christ !!!

"The most important concept one needs to learn is the SWOOPING HAWK or HORUS. The IRON ROD which emanates from the CORE of the Earth points toward the VEGA (=Valley) star in the HARP star constellation. If we do not master that, then we will not understand it." – Thoth claimed.

"The Magnetic North of the Earth's geo-dynamo defines a lot of important concepts, such as the HARP and the HORUS SWOOPING HAWK

151

along with the IRON ROD of the Egyptian Magicians, the IRON ROD of MOSES, KING DAVID, and the Lord, JESUS CHRIST. These varying concepts represent only one thing – the importance of the IRON ROD, that is the MAGNETIC NORTH! Am I right with this conclusion?" – Eva summarized Thoth teachings accurately.

"You nailed it!" – Thoth smiled with a satisfaction of a guru. The mention of conclusion and the teachings of King David created an etheric reaction in the ripples of the timeless space and an unexpected royal visitor emerged.

"G'mar, conclusion?" – we all heard from behind the curtains. - King David walked in unexpectedly. He was carrying the 7–stringed 'kinor' harp. "In my ethereal sleep, suddenly, I sensed that someone needed my musical talent. I am known as the Sweet Singer of Israel." King David proclaimed.

"I know it was not King Saul, who called for me, but someone who needed me to sing the song that would carry us into the WORLD TO COME!" – King David stood there proudly. "Who is asking me, was it you my brother Thoth?" – King David was asking, standing tall and ready to perform his celestial duties. He was young and dashingly good looking. His white satin toga was almost full length reaching below the knees and ribbed style with a wide golden laced belt. The gilded belt had three horizontal layers running above each other. The middle layer had some black letter looking designs in it, likely some importance to him. Over the expansive looking white toga, he had a purple red robe with gilded patterns decorating the edges of his cape. Two Lions decorated the robe, one on each side. The brown leather sandal was not decorated, but the expansive workmanship shown through. From his leather necklace string a leather pouch was hanging down with something inside. The front of the pouch was decorated with the two letters signifying life and standing for Chai and the numerical value of 18 for the two letters from the Gematria.

"Do You desire me to play a sacred song?" – King David offered as he lifted his portable lyre off the ground. The toga and the cape covered up a well-built muscular body.

Eva and I looked at each other with wonder sparkling from our eyes. We could not believe that we were witnessing the miracle that was unfolding in front of our eyes.

'Who could experience something so special in their earthly lives?' – we thought with overflowing happiness.

The scene changed behind King David and now he was walking on the beach front somewhere in the northern part of Israel. The water was bluish green, almost the color of jade. The white foam was rolling up onto the sand in a geometric pattern.

"Did you invent the lyre King David?" – Eva yelled over to his majesty.

King David looked up and answered a straight 'No'. – "But Apollo did." As soon as King David said the words, Apollo appeared on the imaginary beach in front of us carrying his special lyre.

"It is a Cosmic Lyre." – Apollo exclaimed. He was holding up in his hand a small golden colored instrument. "One day I was walking on the beach, and I brushed up against a large turtle shell. The sinew of the turtle shell began to vibrate and that is how I discovered this magical instrument." – Apollo, the father of Orpheus proudly told the old story. "I offered the lyre, my new discovery to Zeus, and asked him for forgiveness for stealing his cows. The cosmic secret of the Orion Nebula relation to the Magnetic and Polar North are hidden in it." Apollo continued with a twisted smile. "He accepted it. It became the sacred lyre and it developed into the harp." – Apollo boasted. "My son, Orpheus is the best virtuoso with the harp." Apollo continued. - "My son Orpheus was so talented and his music so enchanted that his songs had magical effect on everything around him. His songs could even charm the rocks and rivers."

"Thank you, thank you!" – Thoth screamed at Apollo with warmth. "You can all go now!" He instructed those mythological giants. "Too much ego Orpheus! … Okay, let us look at the dynamo."

"So, the ancient Egyptian knew this scientific knowledge, … How come we forgot it?" – I asked.

"The ruling elite in any of these ancient cultures did not want you to know the exact meanings because then they lose control of the masses. They need you to work, be obedient and not to think about these cosmic secrets." – Thoth explained.

"Vega means 'Valley' in Spanish, how did that change to the valley from the 'Hawk'? "

"Okay, sit back close your eyes and I am going to tell you some stories." – Thoth took a deep breath and began. – "The Greeks and the Romans took the Egyptian cosmic mysteries and retained a lot of good information, but also butchered too many important astronomical knowledges. They may have done this on purpose at some junctures. You probably both remember that Cleopatra seduced Julius Caesar and they had a son Caesarion together. Caesarion, also known as Ptolemy, XV ruled together with Cleopatra from 2nd of September 44 BC until her death in 30 BC. Then she seduced Marcus Aurelius. Her first son, Caesarion was the last living male pharaoh and he died as a child. Maybe you or your son lived that kind of royal life in the past?" – Thoth Hermes stared at me with such intensity I had to look away.

"Right Miss Cleopatra?" – he now fixed his eyes on Eva. We were both shocked and did not know how to answer.

"You at least remember the story from the history books?" – Thoth Hermes Trismegistus fixed his eyes on Eva this time.

We both nodded in agreement. We knew the story from our studies.

"What do we need to recall?" – Eva asked.

Thoth Hermes Trismegistus kept staring at us with a piercing look to see if I understood this story. It felt like He thought that I somehow should have remembered some aspects of this as a personal memory. He looked at me to see if I 'really' understood. Well, I did not. The only other time when I felt the spiritual 'eye' of a deity digging deep down to my soul was the day my family and I started driving to a Lakota Sundance from Denver. That was a story that was needed to be remembered another time. Thoth aka Mercury Hermes Trismegistus kept looking into my being with such an intensity that I felt that very cold ice crystals started growing inside of me. I know I had a 'Mercurian Mind' for great analysis, but this was too removed from me to understand. Finally, I had to turn away. I did not understand the intense historical moment he wanted me to recall. Eva responded in a similar fashion. Thoth shook his head in disbelief then continued.

"So, Cleopatra being the last adult powerful Pharaoh Princess or Queen of the Egyptian Empire decided to bring the sacred cosmic knowledge over to Rome that was the new powerhouse." – Thoth squinted toward Eva like she was Cleopatra.

"Did she succeed?" – Eva inquired.

"She did! She accomplished that a few decades before Christ born. Within years Julius Caesar got murdered in the Senate, Cleopatra died by the 'snake suicide' on August 12 in the year 30 BC, his son Cesarion was killed later, on the order of Octavian who later became Augustus." – Hermes again peered at me so intensely that I began to have my ears ringing loud. "Remember this?"

"I cannot relate to the last male pharaoh, who was Cleopatra's son from Julius, but I love the story of Augustus, the First Emperor of peace of the Roman Empire." – I felt the need to state that as He kept looking. I added. "I studied Him at length."

"I bet you did. … That might explain your drive to name your son Austin, which would be a derivative of Augustine." – Thoth was mysteriously smiling at me as he was analyzing my past lives in my soul.

"Then you married Eva from the middle of Europe, who looked like Cleopatra with pitched black straight hair." – Thoth was probing my life and my choices in love. He reminded me of a Freudian psychologist with a twisted mind and the knowledge of several past live regressions. I was not ready to engage him in the thousands of years of battle where family units of spirits return in different roles in the bigger groups to battle out some inequity they experienced in the past.

"I don't think those choices are closely related." – I stated.   He began to talk again but I missed the beginning of his teachings as an old wound was burning a large hole into my everlasting spirit.

"… and the Library of Alexandria in Egypt burnt up. The valuable books were taken to Rome, where the seeds of the Vatican were established based on the ancient cosmic knowledge." – Thoth reported without showing emotion. "Now, the Roman politicians and religious leaders began a systematic destruction of the Egyptian knowledge from the masses. The 'Vega star' that was known to the ancient Persian astronomers as the SWOOPING HAWK - became known as the VALLEY. The famous Egyptian town, the home of Horus the Hawk was known as 'Washty' as the English explorers wrote it down, but it was originally named VASTŐ, which means 'IRON ROD'. That is the secret of the Magnetic North's direction. The Greeks over 2,000 years ago renamed it Thebes and that is how it got famous in Greco-Roman and western civilization." – Thoth looked up and wondered. "…Thebes? … is a fake name."

"When Jesus Christ mentioned that He will give the IRON ROD of rulership to those who behave to His likings, that meant something. That contained a deep cosmic mystery of the Earth's geo-dynamo." –

5.

Two dates everywhere

"The two great black holes that we always want to bring to your attentions is the Orion and Cygnus on the Orion Cygnus Arm of the Milky Way Galaxy. September 17th and March 26, 3 and ½ years apart." – Thoth continued his valuable education. "The eruption of Cygnus X-3 marked re-creation. Cygnus is also known as the Black Swan, the Goose or the Northern Cross." – Thoth said. - "If you do not understand this then you will not understand the true Leonardo Da Vinci secret." We both looked lost. "Pope Julius II asked Leonardo to paint the picture of Leda and the Swan, where Zeus turns into a bird to be able to visit the married Spartan Queen Leda. You will see that later from Pope Julius II himself. Okay, I show you another picture where it shows the eruption from the Virgin." – Hermes Trismegistus aka Thoth offered. "This is the Milky Way Virgin in Egypt. At her head is Orion – that is best seen in September and in her Womb is the Cygnus Swan on March 26. These two black holes switch the climate. To make you understand better, I will ask others to show you these dates as we progress with our studies." - Thoth offered.

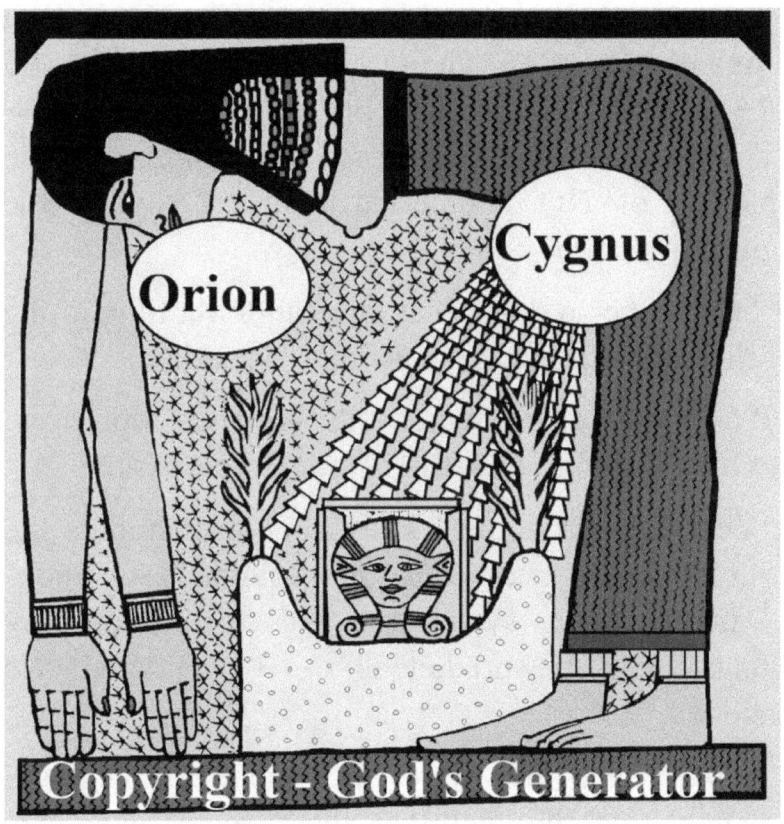

"This eruption happened March 26th, 5786 years ago to 2026, when the next eruption is due. We will teach you both about the cosmic mysteries that underlie the holidays." – He said. – "This is the secret about the Passover story. The Exodus was the human cover story. I will have Rabbi Moses explain it when the time comes." – Thoth seemed to enjoy detecting the confusion on our comically appearing faces. Re-Creation happened 5,786 years ago to the special year 2026. The Hindu Kali Juga ends in 2025. The Great Reset is in 2025 and Re-Creation can happen on March 26, 2026." – Thoth stated with confidence still holding up the picture of Nut (Sumerian Anu / 'Anyu'), the Galactic Virgin.

"Can it be so exact that one can tell a time in the future according to past events?" – I asked.

"Can you tell me when the Sun rises tomorrow, two weeks from now?" – Thoth Hermes asked.

Yes, the astronomers know the exact minute the Sun comes up everyday from past data." – I said. - "Thus, a larger system, such as the Milky Way galaxy can be predicted?" – I wondered. He nodded.

"Okay, let us start the parade. We will demonstrate the fact that these secret dates are everywhere around you, - and you could not recognize them." – Thoth Hermes was stating confidently. "Let me start with the money." – Thoth offered. "On the ONE DOLLAR BILL on one side you see the HEAD of George Washington. The HEAD is CEPHEUS. The star constellation CEPHEUS is where you find the largest black hole S5 0014+ 81 in the vicinity of the Center of the Universe. Then on the other side we have the two secret markers for the two black holes, Orion, and Cygnus. These represent the dates September 17 and March 26. You see the one dollar bill every day." – Hermes Mercury stated.

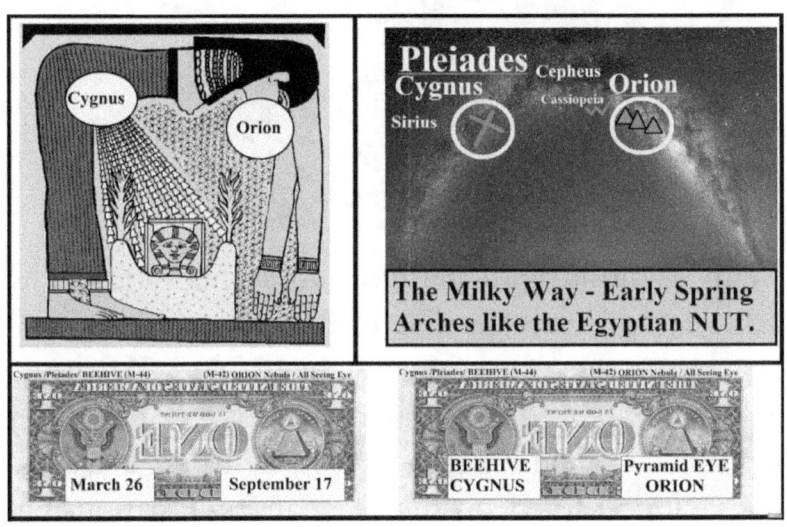

"This pyramid with the Eye represents Orion. The All-Seeing Eye is the Eye of the Galactic Virgin. It represents the day of September 17th, 5,786 years ago when the Orion Nebula erupted 9 months after Christmas. Then 4 years later both the Cygnus and the Orion erupted on the Day of Re-Creation. On the pyramid you see the Roman numerals 1776. That is exactly 250 years away from 2026. That is how the Founding Fathers honed you into these important cosmic dates." – Thoth explained.

"Our religious leaders did not warn?" – I said.

"Pope Julius II warned us for both dates 500 years ago. So, even your religious leaders tried to educate you about those two dates." – Thoth replied.

"This was painted by Michelangelo, on the order of Pope Julius II, depicting the September 17th event 2 cycles ago." – Thoth educated me again.

"Why two cycles ago?" – Eva asked.

"That was the time of the sinking of Atlantis 11,600 years ago. The background behind God is the Orion Nebula brain. Same as the eye on the pyramid on the One Dollar bill." – Thoth stated.

"That is incredible. They did not even have telescopes back then." – I wondered. – "How were they able to maintain a high level of cosmic knowledge in the Dark Ages?" – I wondered.

"Then look at this next painting. Leda and the Swan. This is a copy, but the original was done by

Leonardo da Vinci, on the order of the same Pope Julius II 500 years ago." – Thoth Hermes informed us. This represents the Cygnus SWAN black hole eruption that happened March 26th and was the day of Re-Creation." – Thoth Hermes Trismegistus informed us.

"Isn't it depicting bestiality? How come the Pope promotes these kinds of immoral acts?" – I asked.

"Now, again you are thinking human and animal gods, but this is straight Astronomy and Cosmology. Leda is your Milky Way goddess. She gets impregnated by the CYGNUS SWAN, which is also the Northern CROSS. A great Pope, like Julius could have not been clearer on this – emphasizing Astronomy." – Thoth explained.

"It is only another proof that your ancient religious and political leaders knew about the cosmic secrets, opened it up to you – granted, without proper education and explanations. But the masses would have killed them. The Dark Ages were brutal to the Astronomers." – Thoth explained history.

"Why do we have four babies born out the eggs?" – Eva asked.

"That is the number of eruptions that happened around March 26th. The first cosmic Passover and Easter celebration. Now at least you start understanding the secrets of the Easter Bunny and the decorated eggs." – Thoth smiled gently.

"Okay, I begin to see the eggs tied to Easter, but why would they need to be decorated with lines of resonations and colors?" – my wife wondered.

"The secret is in the hieroglyphic spelling of the 'Ankh' ('AnyuKő') where the 'vase' that is positioned in the womb of Nut, shows these resonations. It is right now very advanced knowledge you do not have to know, but the Egyptian 'N' resonation and the hot gas bubbles appearing in the sky with different colors, … that is what the elaborate decoration of the eggs represent." – Thoth explained. - "Your Magyar tribe, along with the Vikings, called the Pleiades star constellation the 'Hen with Chicks'? Now, then you ask yourself, 'What came first the Hen or the chick? It is an elaborate way to remember Re-Creation at Easter. This complexity is not for the simpletons." – Thoth explained. "To connect all those strange stories and star constellations to actual cosmic events is very difficult. It forces humanity to evolve to be smarter." – Thoth concluded.

"Are there more evidence for these two dates?" – I asked knowing that the answer will be affirmative.

"The Egyptian Dendera Zodiac astronomy ceiling picture is the most ancient star map of all." – Thoth stated. "It also marks those two points."

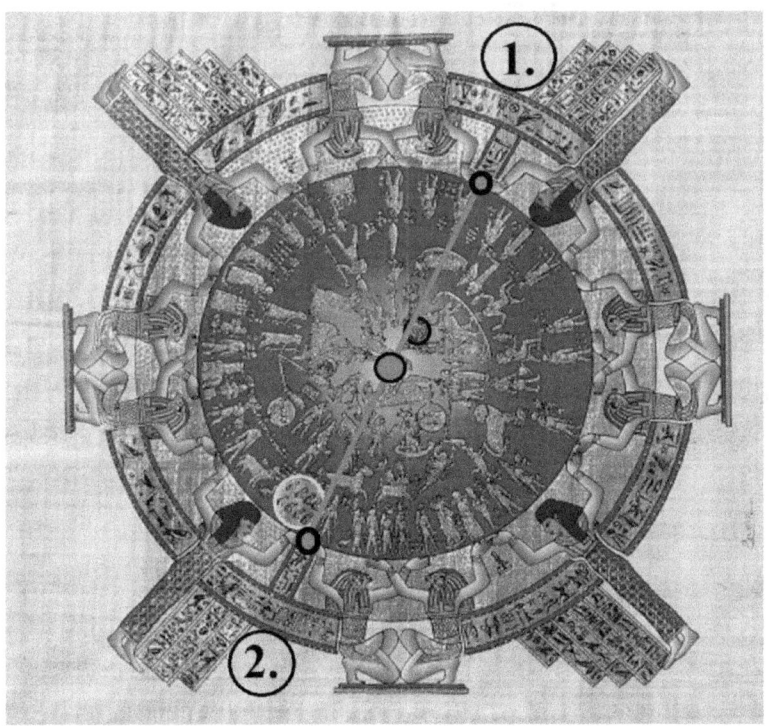

"Here on the picture of the Dendera Zodiac we can see at # 1 is the March 26th date of Re-Creation at around 1 o'clock." – Thoth informed us. Then # 2 is the September 17th date." – Hermes informed us.

"I still don't understand how come we have this astronomical art history in front of our eyes, and we cannot decipher these dates?" – I wondered.

"Well son, it is even worse. When you wake up out of your magical dream, you can go to the Wikipedia and find these dates mentioned. The Washington Monument was built to place a shadow on the Congress door twice a year; September 17th and March 26th. Josephus Africanus 2,000 years ago stated that the early Christians celebrated the Day of Creation and New Year on March 26th. I could go on and on. Your teachers, politicians and religious leaders displayed these astronomical dates in front of you everywhere, but you had to solve the riddles. The Dark Ages were so brutal on the knowledge of Astronomy that everybody who knew the star knowledge were afraid to reveal it. It was done in secret meetings, so the angry mobs would not kill them off. Enough for now, I want you to prepare to enter one of the gates of the Hall of Truth where you will get most of your education. We will pick you two guides who will navigate you through the maze and two other guides will follow in the shadows." – Thoth concluded.

"I volunteer to be one of those guides for Eva." – a nice male voice came from the East as he walked in wearing a well-tailored suit. It was L. Ron Hubbard the Founder of the Church of Scientology. A prolific writer who put out hundreds, if not thousands of books, articles, essays about important subjects. To his credit, he was very worried about the destructive power of nuclear fusion, which we passionately shared with him. Besides that, he was committed to teach humanity how to become better souls in a challenging world. He was a genius.

"Thank You Master for teaching so many incredible wisdoms." – Eva was very happy.

"You know when I passed – I mean my body passed and separated from my everlasting spirit in this Earthly life in 1986 there was no black hole knowledge. The geo-dynamo model came out in 1994 and Stephen Hawkins, one of the experts on black holes was still arguing about CYGNUS X-1 not being a black hole. So, no wonder that in my earthly human life I could not venture into the ideas of black holes. They were not in the consciousness of the population." – Hubbard explained.

"Do You believe in re-incarnation Master?" – Eva inquired.

"I definitely do. When I was younger, I had a near-death experience and that event reassured me that we exist in this Universe forever. God gave us an everlasting Spirit from Himself and with that we travel through time and take on new human forms. Our body does not want to pass easily, but if we know that spirit lives, it is easier. We constantly learn from one life to another." – Hubbard stated.

Thoth stood up from His throne and waved to Mr. Hubbard.

"Ron, you have been an inspiration for millions. I will ask you to be one of Eva's guides – but for now only in the background. She will have two female guides that are already chosen. Once we go and pass the Axis Shift of 2026, there will be a Grand Reset as you already know. In the reset the females will become males and the males will be assigned to be females. That is when the positive turns negative and the negative switches to positive. A magnetic shift will happen throughout the whole Universe. You can prepare Eva for that and explain to her telepathically why the Egyptian female Red Hyena was chosen by her Sumerian ancestors to represent the shift. Stay in the background and you will take your place as a guide after the magnetic reset of the genders." – Thoth waved again. This time it meant for him to become invisible to us. Eva and I looked at each other and smiled. This was a good moment meeting giants who walked on Earth before us.

"Did you know Cutie, that the spotted Egyptian female Red Hyena is the only canine that has a false penile shaft protecting her private part?" – I asked my wife. Strangely, the voice that came out of my mouth was the voice of Hubbard.

"Did you say something?" – my wife asked me.

"What?" – I felt confused. I looked at my wife and we both chuckled.

"So, the brilliant Sumerian Egyptian scientists of Astronomy and Cosmology again picked an animal to represent the Cygnus X-3 eruption with the spots, just as the Bambi deer would have those spots. The red color is the color of the Red Cloud. Being a hyena who eats dead animal carcasses have another enigma attached to this creature. Then, with the false penile shaft it marks the changing from a female to the male. That is brilliant." – Eva rattled off what came to her mind. "Now, I see why the British Royals are so much into hunting for the Red Fox. That was the European version of the Egyptian hyena." – She was laughing out loud.

"Who picks our guides?" – I was curious and ready to move on to the gates.

"You both already picked them in your spirits, you just don't know, yet." – Thoth replied.

6.

Hall of Truth

Eva and I were standing in front of seven doors on the East wall of the large waiting room. From the North side Thoth entered with a person who radiated so much light that it felt like the energy of 10,000 suns. It was a soft and warm feeling, but we sensed that given the right circumstances it can burn us into ashes. As He approached, we started recognizing Him. It was the LORD, Jesus Christ, God Himself coming toward me. I almost fainted.

"Lord, foremost Son of God – would You please dampen your radiance so these earthly humans can withstand your presence." – Thoth asked God politely in His most recognizable human form.

"Stand up straight Willy, the Lord wants to look into your eyes." – my wife urged me.

I followed her command and stood up tall. The Lord stepped up close to me and I could feel his white robe gently push some refreshing air toward me. I was fully energized. On a deeper level in real life - it felt that I was on a ventilator intubated and someone was shining a bright light into my eyes.

"You have good intentions. Willy, you will do great learning and discovery on this journey." – The Lord exclaimed after he spent what felt like an eternity looking into my eyes. -" I am looking at your two black pupils, as if they were two black holes. It allows me to look into your soul that leads all the way to the Father." – Jesus explained.

"Lord, I am a sinner." – I started into my usual pious prayer.

"Leave these thoughts out of here Son." – Jesus Christ sternly instructed me. "One cannot see the Truth once they always feel guilty. Guilt is not allowed here on this journey. … And don't call me Lord. Here in the Hall of Truth it has bad connotation. It means the destructive gas bubbles."

"Okay then Excellency, how should we address You?" – I asked as I looked over to Eva to see if she has a better idea.

"J.C. will do it up here." The Lord stated.

"J.C. will be one of your guides." – Thoth offered.

"Thank You Thoth." – I felt very honored. "Who will be the second one?" – I asked after a moment of hesitation to avoid being overwhelmed.

"Voila." – a voice resonated from the direction of the North Gate. A human shaped mountain goat walked in. "I am Satan." – he proudly announced.

"Satan? But … I don't want you as a guide with your sins around me." – I protested loudly. Pain began to generate in my body as I resisted.

"Relax son and the pain will leave you. TRUTH has two components, GOOD and BAD. If you cannot handle the Truth with good and bad, you will not be able to complete the training here." – Satan smiled pleasantly. The horns on the top of his head were not threatening. I looked over to Thoth who was smiling. I peered over to the Lord to see if He would approve. He was just looking at me with a neutral stare signifying that the decision was mine.

"Okay. If that is what I need to learn, I will do it. … Thank You Mr. Satan for volunteering to be my guide." – I changed my attitude.

"Of course." – Satan replied. "Call me Sata, without that resonating 'N' for now." I nodded in agreement. "One more thing so you understand how I was named Sata in Egypt. I will show you the Egyptian hieroglyphic spelling of my name so you can guess what I am about." – Sata smiled mysteriously.

"That will reveal something secretive?" – Eva butted in uninvited.

"Yes, you tell me if my name will give you clarity about the Cosmos." – Satan posed.

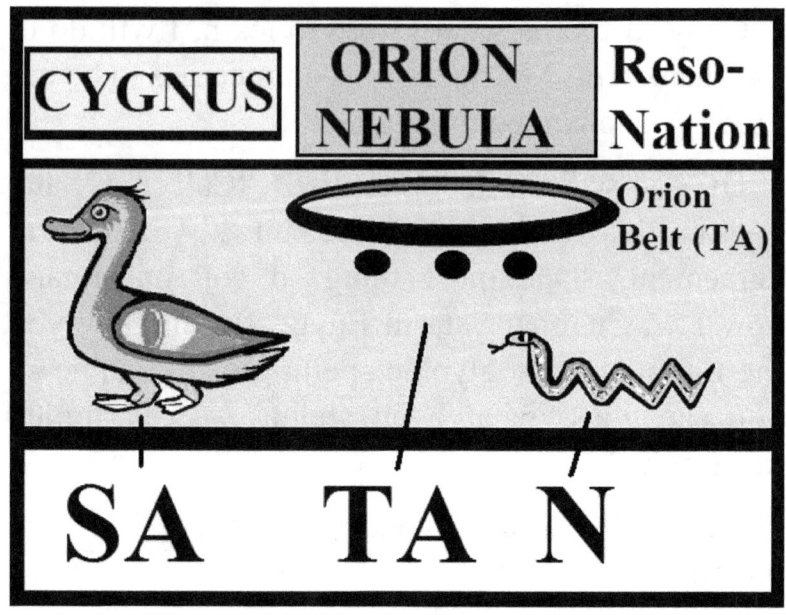

"Here is the Egyptian hieroglyphic spelling of my name the SA-TA Serpent. This is where you derive the name Satan. Just let us look at it and I want you two to analyze what you see and tell me who I am." – Sata was challenging our knowledge of the Egyptian hieroglyphic alphabet, along with the cosmic secrets behind it.

"The first biliteral Egyptian letter is 'SA'. That is the Goose or elsewhere the Swan. It is also the same astronomically as the NORTHERN CROSS, CYGNUS." – I stated it to show my knowledge. Suddenly it hit me. "Wait!" – I shouted it out loud. "Satan you have the Cygnus Cross in your name?"

"Now you are talking!" – Sata laughed out loud. "So, just a minute ago you did not want to have me as a guide and now you are connecting me to the sacred Cross in the Womb of the Milky Way goddess. ... Jesus Christ!" – He trumpeted.

"So, after the Cygnus / Northern Star constellation in the first part of your name, what else we should notice?" – I was a little annoyed.

"I can easily tell you that." – Eva chimed in. "The 'TA' part of your name resembles the Belt of Orion - and the 3 stars are either, the belt stars or the 3 sword stars. That would tie you to the Orion Nebula black hole." – my wife extended her arms explaining it.

"That is weird Sata. Your name represents the two most important BLACK HOLES on the Cygnus Orion Arm of our Galaxy. Are you then part of Re-Creation?" – I was totally baffled.

"So, apparently ... J.C. was born out of the Orion Nebula black hole and then He was re-born at Easter from the Cygnus black hole. ... and He is the good guy." – Sata had a hint of disappointment in his voice. "Then I am also connected to the Orion Nebula and the Cygnus black holes, but ... "Sata hesitated. "... I guess, I got the part - in this strange Cosmic Comedy – the role of the bad guy, like always." - Sata appeared genuinely disappointed.

Both Eva and I looked at each other and felt sad about this creature. We always hated him with a passion, we blamed him for the ills of the world, and now here we are … feeling empathy for Satan.

"That is the feeling I wanted to ingrain in you." – Sata cheered up mischievously. "I just wanted you to understand that both of us … "- he looked over toward J.C. for approval. Christ was listening with eyes closed, seemingly in a deep meditation. "… we both are about teaching the Cosmic Truth. That truth involves the two black holes on the Cygnus Orion Arm of the Galaxy where our Solar System is. These two black holes give us life and occasionally take it away. You cannot believe in God's eternal design if you do not want to know the Truth. The truth – in your minds can be good or bad – but truly, it is just the Truth. We are both here to teach you that." – Sata completed his sermon. We remained solemnly quiet. The lack of sounds for a minute seemed like eternity, but it allowed us to have these deep thoughts sink into our consciousness.

"So, both of my guides are about the two mythological black holes." – I quietly mumbled to myself, nobody seemed to care to notice.

"The Sacred Cross in the sky, who is the beautiful Swan, and the belt of Orion is me!" – Satan playfully sang his own praise.

"So, why do they often show you as a goat?" – came the obvious question from Eva.

"Oh, that is easy. Go back to the Dendera Zodiac picture. When the Orion Nebula erupted in the past, it happened the second time at the end of September. When one looks up the sky toward the Polaris, it is when the Capricorn - mountain goat is on the ecliptic path of the Sun. That is why I became known as the devil who looks like a goat. Also, because I poured the water from the ocean onto Earth, they depicted me as half-fish half goat. This then became the water pouring ceremony of the Jewish New Year. Everything is connected." – Sata proudly looked up. He was happy he could teach us some astronomy and cosmology. "Now, you hopefully begin to understand the passages of the Bible in Leviticus. That is where the story of the 'scape goat' is being told. The rabbi chooses two goats, one will be sacrificed and the other one will be released to the forest to be free, that's me. The cosmic knowledge background is the event that happened toward the end of September 5,786 years ago. The zodiac sign that begins on September 21st is the SCALE, which is Libra. That 'scale' pulled up the water from the ocean and poured it on the face of the Earth. If we did not start teaching you these seemingly unrelated pictures and events, you would never be able to solve these puzzles." – Satan was teaching us about the mysteries. For the first time in my life and near death, the September 17th event, the large tsunami, the pulling up the water ceremony, the biblical passages, the 'Eye' of the pyramid and millions of related pictures of this cosmic puzzle started to become one important cosmic knowledge. It was all a reminder of the act of God. Our Father God began the process to re-energize the weakening geo-dynamo of the Earth. He showed us the same faith as He asked Abraham to display when his son was almost thrown into the Fire of Nimrod Orion. God will recall almost all the spirits from Earth when this tragedy happens, so He can maintain a few human lives on Earth. These humans will go through the 7 years of Famine and the long years of Tribulation to be the seed of future humanity. If He did not re-energize the magnetic field of the Earth – we would have a lifeless planet Mars on our hand and no more human existence. A thoughtful Father who needs to extinguish life for billions of humans and only allow room underground for a few millions to survive and repopulate our fragile globe. My spirit without a human body contemplated these enigmas. In the awake human flash state - I could not have the wisdom to understand the periodic destruction that was the design of the God King of the Universe. What a love!" – I was daydreaming about this.

"It is your turn." – Thoth turned to Eva. My guides, J.C. and Sata disappeared in thin air for now. I felt less stressed. Finally, I began to grasp that our Almighty God gave us good and bad, which was neither. It was just the COSMIC TRUTH!

"My turn to do what?" – Eva was surprised.

"It is your turn to meet your spiritual guides." – Thoth informed my wife.

7.

The Queen

"Cleopatra is your first guide Eva. She has a long connection to you spiritually and she volunteered to be of help." – Thoth explained. A Liz Taylor looking beauty with soft brown eyes walked into the hallway. The straight black hair was shoulder length, and the typical golden Cobra crown headdress was sprinkling with bright colors.

"Eva my dear, you and I as one will have a fabulous time on this journey." – Cleopatra promised. Her 3 layered tunic was silk black with golden threads and patterns, but so lightly treaded that her bikini style clothing below showed through. The olive skin of her stomach and upper thigh occasionally shined thru as the tunic blew open on quick choreographed theatrical movements. In the real world there would be a lot of sexual chakras opening - but up here at the Edge of the Atmosphere there were no such human forces present.

"I feel very close to you Cleopatra. I am excited about the time I will spend learning from you. Your Cobra head dress teaches me about the Orion eruption, right?" – Eva stated with overflowing confidence. "It was brilliant from You 'sister' that You designed that Cobra Crown. It hangs over your forehead, right over your PINEAL GLAND. So, that means You are the GALACTIC VIRGIN? You are playing out the COSMIC WISDOM with your finely designed jewelries?" – Eva concluded.

"You are exactly right as you already possess all the knowledge subconsciously that I came here to teach you. I am only here to help you dig deeper without fear." – Cleopatra explained.

"What about me?" – Queen Emese, the Founding Magyar Royalty chimed in. It was a surprise that the founding Magyar Queen appeared to my wife.

Queen Emese historically lived just north of the Caucasian Mountains 1,200 years ago after they were pushed out of the Land of Sumer by the newly arriving migrant people. She was dressed in a richly decorated Persian style kaftan that was customary of her time. She was the Queen Mother of Almos ('biblical Amos') and 200 years later the Great-great-great-great Grandmother of the First

Christian ruler of Hungary, Saint Stephen. She was proudly standing there as a hawk was sitting on her right shoulder. The red trapeze shaped crown on her head had sacred cosmic symbols scribbled all over.

"Welcome Queen Emese." – Eva shouted loud.

"Well, I am here. I am your other guide that Thoth assigned to you to be of help navigating the Hall of Truth." – Queen Emese, whose name in the Magyar tongue is announced 'Emeshe' – introduced herself. She was the Magyar version of the Galactic Virgin. From her Womb of the Great Dark Rift a sacred river busted open. The Great Dark Rift where stars are born ran from the Cygnus star constellation of the Womb toward Aquila the Eagle and the Sagittarius A. center of the Galaxy. Queen Emese prophesized that from her sacred womb a long line of kings will be born. The first one was Saint Stephen who was crowned king on December 25th, 1,000 AD. For 300 more years kings were born from that House of Arpad dynasty, that finally died out. The Dream of Emese was complete and short lived. It was now the New Cosmic Time.

"Thank You Queen Emese to be my guide." – Eva rattled it off enthusiastically. My wife pointed at her trapezium shaped crown and the crescent decoration on top of it. - "…and thank you for dressing up in a manner to bring me the cosmic clues about the two black holes. First, I notice the RED TRAPEZIUM CROWN that represent the star constellation of the ORION NEBULA black hole. Then the CRESCENT on top is Barnard's Loop. The Golden Elk is March 26th Re-Creation. The HAWK is the Swooping Hawk of Vega, Magnetic North. Wow"

Looking at the Queen, Eva noticed that her own facial features strongly resembled that of Emese, - and … Cleopatra. It felt like she lived in the body of Cleopatra 2,000 years ago, then later as Queen Emese 1,200 years ago, and now she is here for another time as a simple person to bring back the royal cosmic truths. All the cosmic reminders those queens left behind for her on their dresses and jewelries are now paying off to understand it all. Millions of people, Hollywood movies, books, poems, paintings are finally paying off.

"For some strange reasons Eva, I trust you deep inside my God-given soul. Once you picked the Gate, I will come back to help you." – the Queen along with Cleopatra disappeared in a red mist.

"I will pick a good gate." – my wife was mumbling to herself quietly.

"Let us choose your gate in this Hall of Truth." – Thoth reappeared as soon as the two ladies were gone.

"Okay." – Eva agreed. I felt also ready to go and walk through the Hall of Truth with our special guides and my lovely wife.

"The two of you come with me." – Thoth walked us to the East side where the seven gates were. There was a small gate in the middle that did not look big enough to fit through, but the other 6 gates were wide and spacious. There were 3 gates on each side of the small gate. I know we would not consider the small gate, but we wanted to know what to expect on the other gates.

"Which gate you suggest we pick?" – Eva asked Thoth.

"Well, that is your decision." – Thoth Hermes Trismegistus answered. "The 3 gates on the right are some forms of long-life paths or professional success that you would enjoy. The left 3 gates have variations of strength, beauty, richness, and successfully overcoming the hardship life presents to you. I lot of battles and learning. The middle gate is the one that you would want to avoid due to the extreme hardship it represents." – Thoth explained.

"We agree with that. Learning, but not suffering." – I stated with confidence and Eva agreed with me.

"Okay, go to the gates, read the contents by each gate and pick the best one." – Thoth instructed us.

"Let's go Cutie." – I turned to my wife. We walked up to the first gate on the right. Interestingly, it was marked as # 1. Eva started reading the content on the wall. "What does it say?" – I asked.

"In short. When we do the right thing and comply with God's moral law, we will gain a long healthy life, there will be no hardship and much more blessings." – Eva was summarizing it to me.

"Will our guides come to help us chose the right path for us?" – I asked as I looked above the small gate with angry bees flying out of a beehive.

"I am suspecting it will be up to us, so probably they will not come until we agreed on our entrance." – my wife told me. As we talked the gate opened and people poured out with laughing and happiness. As they were talking about their great experiences, we intently listened in. It was all good news. Eva and I both looked at each other and we felt happy.

We intently listened to the conversations of the people who were pouring through the wide gates.

"I can't believe we live that long. 600 years and I felt like I was maybe 70 years old. I was almost 100 years old when I got married. Awesome biblical times. Can you imagine that."– The young girl asked the others as she walked out of the first gate with 3 other friends. It seemed like there were three couples who also participated in this strange prophet school. There were rolling laughs. The guys were talking to each other about their experiences further away, but the girls remained closer to us.

"I can't believe that at age 120 years old I felt young, and I could run 20 miles a day and barely got out breath." – one of the guys with dark brown hair bragged to the other two.

"Have you guys tried those indigo berries? … I ate two of them and I was not hungry all day. The other thing that surprised me that I can talk to my wife telepathically. I told her how much I loved her without saying a word. She loved me back with all she had for days. I felt so happy that there are no words to describe. I am not afraid from the future anymore after I seen what it could be. It is magic without any suffering or hardship. It felt truly like we were in Heaven." - The dirty blond guy with a goatee beard explained to the other two.

He was talking and was animated with such excitement that Eva and I just could not get enough listening to the voices of these people.

"I think I want to go through the first gate." – Eva admitted to me. I had to agree with her. Both of us were very excited about the future. It will be all happiness and harmony, blessings, and beauty.

We listened to more chatter from the couples.

"I had so much happiness after I found out that I was a genius. Anybody asked me anything, I right away knew the answer. After awhile my wife and I were just sitting there imagining how smart our children will be. She just quietly sat across from me, looking at me with her beautiful brown eyes. I tried to think of what else I can ask her and what could be learnt from me. We already knew that we both had the answers for everything we ever wanted to learn or find out. We were able to go into the ether and I was able to ascend into the fifth dimension." – A redheaded guy with beard emerged from gate 2.

"There was nothing physical to worry about. My wife and I were two spirits. Beautiful colors swirled around like we were floating in a kaleidoscope, and we became united in spirit and we both understood that we were floating toward the Source, the only God who exists in the Universe. I was just one with her and as we floated closer to the higher dimensions, other beings joined in and now I totally lost my individuality. I did not know who I was, but happiness filled me up to such a degree that I could not even comprehend how much joy exists in the world. The higher we progressed in the dimensions the more spirits we fused with. I was one with all. I had no issues, no questions, nothing to know, nothing to question." – the 40 some years old guy with the red beard explained it to the twenty-some years old girl with blue hair, who was hanging onto every word he uttered like he was a new age saint.

"I did not see too much initially, I sat in a well decorated room with insanely beautiful flowers, but after a few hours two tall gray aliens came to me and told me that they have to take me to another galaxy where there were no females. They asked me if I would be their queen and rule over there forever, or at least for a thousand years. It was incredible, anything I even started thinking to ask them to do, they were already on it." – blue hair stated proudly.

"How did they communicate with you, telepathically?" – the slightly rotund red head asked the girl. She nodded enthusiastically.

"Yes, before I could state my wish - they would already complete the task I wanted to ask them to do. … It became a little boring after a few days. I wanted a new tattoo, it appeared on my skin right away." – the blue haired girl with a skinny body bragged.

Another blond lady with a very nice face and almost perfect body walked out of one of the other gates on the left side. "Everywhere I went with my family, there were two angels flying behind us to protect everybody. Anything I prayed for became a reality. The Lord appeared to me several times and assured me that as … I pray with a good heart, everything I wish for will come through." – the pretty blondie explained. "It was perfection."

"Wow!" – Eva turned toward me after we listened in on several other uplifting discussions from the people who exited out of the different gates. The future looked bright, and we did not know what to say. Eva had a look of concern on her face that I recognized already. She was staring into nothing like she had a veil in front of her eyes. She stopped focusing and went into Spirit. I quietly observed from the corner of my eyes to see when she will be back to reality and able to talk to me. Finally, we recovered from the star dust that was sprinkled into our eyes.

"I have not been able to decide which gate to go through. I have so many questions in my mind, … but now it feels useless to ask them. I feel reassured that the future is bright." – I explained to Eva who seemed less enthusiastic.

"Did you hear those people, they were so happy, full of exciting events. Going through one of these gates will enrich our lives and understanding of how the perfect Universe works on different levels. If we figure out how the Red Cloud Prophecy will fit into the future and how we can make the world a better place, we can become prophets of good news." – I tried to explain my reasoning to my wife.

She usually liked situations that were happy ending, so I did not understand why she was not happier. "You know there are so many prophets and ministers who are the bringers of the 'good news', I am not sure I trust this bright future. Maybe that is the 'good news' what we bring to the people, but I wonder if there is bad news also, … that we ignore and will not be able to prepare for that." – Eva explained herself. I followed her stare fixating in the middle section of the gates with the beehive.

"You're not thinking of going through the narrow gate?" – I asked with some concerns.

"No, no way." – Eva answered nervously with swift speed. "We cannot even fit through."

"Okay." – I said. I looked away, because I started having some doubts myself that I can handle all the 'good news' and then there is nothing to prepare for in case some tragedy approaches. How can one choose between good and bad when there are only good and positive things flowing out of the pickets of the giving Universe? - I thought. "I will not be able to separate the good, as there will be no polarity to compare."

"You know, … I was thinking." - Eva admitted. "If Santa Claus, Thoth, Jesus Christ, Cleopatra, and others want us to complete our training, … it does not make sense." – my wife posed.

"What do you mean?" – I asked.

"If only good things will flow out of the Universe in the future, why are we needed? As goodness flows, we can just passively accept - all the gifts that God gives us. There is no need for prophet school." – Eva summarized her thoughts. Before I could answer her, our four guides reappeared right next to us, reassuringly surrounding the two of us.

"I am glad you made your decisions. You remembered my teaching." – Lord J.C. stated with happiness. We both looked at Him not understanding what He meant. "Walk through the narrow gate!" – Jesus repeated His old teaching.

"Wow, I remember now." – I realized. "But … what about those angry bees? I swell up bad after the sting of the bee." – I continued my complaining. JC was staring at me without any emotions. "Okay, not like I will need an Epipen, but it is … serious." I explained less and less convincingly.

Jesus Christ was standing in all His glamour without moving a facial muscle. I began to feel a reassuring strength emanating from my Savior.

"Those bee stings, … they are not even that bad, they just itch for days." – I was turning away looking down to see how I can escape from my negativity.

"If that happens, we can just put some apple cider vinegar on it." – Eva offered. Her training was as a Master Herbologist and Master Iridologist. In real life she was my doctor, not the other way around.

"Okay, we are all good?" – a cheery Sata was asking us. We all nodded in agreement. "Can we enter into the Hall of Truth then?" – he asked.

"Yes." – my wife answered loudly. I nodded but had my doubts. I don't like the bee stings.

"Okay, as we go inside, we will walk the history lane and after every station we will have a stop in the auditorium to discuss the subjects. That is when you can ask your questions. If the events become too scary for your spirit to handle, you can step out through the side window to disengage. It will take all of us out there with you. We are entering the most gruesome possible scenario that can happen to humanity. It does not have to become reality, but this will be the worse, possible scenario that can happen to any one of you." -Sata calmly explained.

Remembering how I let Eva enter the unknown the last time, I offered to go first.

"I cannot fit through this opening." – I was complaining as I tried to squeeze my fat body through the narrow opening of the middle gate with all the bees. Eva gave me a push. I fell through. I stood up and it was like I was standing on top of a hill watching something in a distance with a binocular. My wife entered in and remarked.

"I think we eat too much" – she said as she was dusting off her princess outfit.

"We do eat a lot. Where are the guides?" – I asked.

"They are spirits, they can fly through the wall I guess." – Eva remarked as she was looking behind herself and not seeing anybody.

"What were you watching with those binoculars? Where did you get them anyway?" – Cutie had more questions than answers. Whenever she was disturbed in a situation, I noticed that she would ask me all these questions coming out of her mouth like a rapid-fire machine gun.

"I don't know." – I looked down to my right hand that was holding the binoculars. I felt guilty possessing a thing that was not mine, so I handed it over to her in a hurry. "Here you take it." – I passed the problem on to her.

"Wait, this is Christmas 2022 coming up in a few days, the street sign said it." – I told her as we were walking toward the tallest peak of the mountain.

"Did you hear that?" – my wife asked me.

"Hear what?" – I was startled in my deep thinking as I walked with my head down as if I was a quarter horse.

"Croak, croak." – the sounds got louder and louder. Huge frogs by the thousands were surrounding us in an instance and more were coming up from the valleys.

"Where did they come from?" – I asked more surprised than scared.

"From all over." – my wife proclaimed being annoyed by the slimy creatures. We looked down toward the valley and putrid water was standing in the lower elevations.

"Perfect breeding ground for these creatures." – I remarked.

"You know, it is the time of Kwanza, Channukah, Christmas and these creatures make the scenery appear like the beginning of the biblical plaques." – Eva was stating the obvious.

"Are you hot, and sweating too?" – I was asking my wife. "Where is the heat coming from at the end of December? It's crazy!" – I proclaimed.

"Yes. I am hot, too." – Cutie just realized that I was wiping my face with my arms like they were windshield wipers.

"It is almost Christmas, … it should not be this hot." – I complained. The smaller frogs began to climb into my pants from below and I felt very uncomfortable with the heat and the slime. I was pretty sure they won't bite me, but I still felt creepy.

"So many mosquitos and they are huge." – Eva nervously slapped the side of her neck and her arm. I started running up the hill dragging her with me and not looking back. The drone-sized mosquitos fell behind and we caught a good break. When we ran what seemed like a whole week, we got up to the top of the mountain and it was very peaceful. We sat down and rested for a few minutes. Nostalgia sneaked in on us.

"Today is December 24th Christmas Eve. I looked at my imaginary wristwatch. It is almost 5 o'clock in the afternoon. … Cutie, do you remember that we met and started dating on Christmas Eve 1976?" – I asked my wife.

"That was a long time ago. I don't feel that old." – Eva proclaimed.

"Exactly 45 years ago. I just finished high school a few months before and I found you." – I stated it with a hint of nostalgia.

"And now we will be watching the after effect of the Orion Nebula eruption. If it is 2022 that we have missed the first eruption last Christmas and the huge tsunami at the end of September. So, this is what we will experience after the tsunami poured over the land. … I don't feel like 45 years passed." - Eva looked at her body and shook her head. She did not like those numbers. In her own mind she was 39 years old and how could 45 years pass. The math did not add up in her brain.

"Look!" – I looked up and pulled the binoculars out of her hand. It was getting darker, and it almost looked like that there was a light shining from the Sword of Orion in the sky.

"It's not dark enough to see." = Eva said.

"Let's then take a nap and then we wake up in the middle of the night we will see the stars better." – I suggested.

"I'm already sleeping." – my wife leaned back on the comfortable rocking chair that appeared underneath her. I noticed also that I have a rocking chair. I started feeling very happy. It is Christmas Eve, children around the world are going to sleep with the thoughts that when they wake up there will be so many gifts wrapped under the Christmas Tree that it will be immensely joyful to unwrap them. Gifts that they expected and more gifts that they could not imagine. It is a special day of the year to remember. What a glorious night. We slept a lot and when I woke up the sign said that we are at Christmas 2021. Maybe when I fell, we progressed a year ahead to 2022. Now we are back at the beginning at Christmas of 2021.

"What was that?" – I screamed out loud. A scorpion must have stung me. Then another one.

"What is your problem …?" – my wife began to ask me as I woke her from her comfort, but she ended up screaming from the pain of the scorpion stings herself. Hundreds of those creatures descended on our bodies, climbing up from the ground. I looked down and could not see my ankle as the scorpions covered my skin. Eva was also covered with them Nothing we could do. The vicious stings of the scorpions caused a burning pain all over my body. I hurt so much the burning was so immense that I began to scream my prayer out to the Lord. I felt that I will pass out unless I pray hard.

"Take me Lord! I am ready to die. My body cannot exist on Earth one more minute with this intense burning pain. I looked over to Eva who was shouting like a killing pig. For a second, I remembered that sound of the squeal that the pig gave out when the country folks got of hold of them. The pig still had a faint hope though that somehow, maybe he can escape the slaughter and disappear into the depth of the forest to later reemerge as a wild boar and gore the evil humans to death. That was not an option for us. Eva and I were screaming from the top of our lungs trying to get relief from the burning pain. I was hurting so much that I was passing in and out of consciousness. Death now would have been a welcome relief.

I looked over to Eva. She was shaking violently and screaming obscenities. That was not her. I was crying rivers out of my eyes, I wanted to help but I was paralyzed from the stings of the scorpions. The impotent feeling that I could not move and act to be of help to the one I loved the most, who suffered in front of me was the worst feeling anybody could experience. Thousands of years of suffering, rape, wars, injury, betrayal, burning on the stake, falling into the bottom of dark caves full of rotting corpses were flickering in front of my eyes as a bad horror movie. I knew I was going to die, but I hoped it would come sooner than later. Pain can be very demoralizing. I was hallucinating so much from the pain that I began to see things that were not there. A huge wild boar appeared in the sky. It had huge tusks. It was floating toward Mother Earth. I could read the mind of this beast. He was looking at the globe like if it was a female boar. One that was in heat and was full of desire. The celestial male wild boar decided to have passionate sex with the female boar, except it was our Mother Earth and not a female pig as the floating beast imagined. I wanted to yell out to the boar and tell him that if he makes love to Mother Earth, it will cause earthquakes and volcanoes to erupt. The evil smile of this beast with the enormous tusks told me that even if I could oink in pig language, he would not understand it.

"Oink, oink the pig!" – Eva looked at me as the first shaking of the Earth happened. The pain and the burning disappeared from our bodies, and we felt human again. The scorpions retreated there were no needs for the hammock to protects us from the scorpions. Our rocking chairs stopped swaying back and forth.

"Why is this happening?" – I asked Cutie. She smiled mysteriously before she started explaining it. While I was in my deep thoughts and meditation before the attack from the scorpions, she managed to visit up with the elves of the forest who were mostly invisible to us, but occasionally we would see some shadows passing in the corners of our eyes.

"How are you doing?" – my wife asked.

I did not know what to say. I was happy that the burning pain left my body but now I felt exhausted and just wanted to sleep. "Okay" - I lied.

As soon as I closed my eyes the slumbering sleep that would overcome even a bear hit me.

"Are you up?" – Cutie touched my shoulder.

"Now, I am." – I was yawning as I tried to wake up from a deep sleep. I looked around and the stars were still up. My wristwatch showed that it was already the next evening, December 25th, 2021.

"We slept through Christmas?" – I was surprised.

"It was the darkest day I remember." – Cutie stated. "I woke up, it was so dark, it looked like the Sun became like the color of sackcloth and I went back to sleep. I dreamt that we were stung by scorpions, and we were burning up with heat and insanity." – she spoke funny, as it sounded like she was talking out of concha seashell.

"How come you didn't wake me up. … What is that noise coming from the sky?" – I was disturbed. The rocking chairs were rocking underneath us as if the Earth moved back and forth a few inches at a time. Mother Earth was rocking us as if we were her babies.

"Look, there is a ruddy colored red cloud on the East behind our dark Sun." – Eva sounded more enthusiastic than I was prepared for.

"Which way is East?" – I was still not fully awake.

"Orient yourself. It is in the ORIENT!" – Eva emphasized with a slight sarcasm in her voice. That was not her style. I was known as the sarcastic one. The realization that the ancient built the 'orientation' word into our language to tie it to the East woke me up. It was mental stimulation. Thus, I oriented myself to the Orient to see Orion. I looked toward the East and out of the Red Cloud appeared Christ in a white tunic walking in the sky.

"Wow, what is that apparition?" – I asked.

The picture in my mind looked like Michelangelo's 'Creation of Adam' painting. God was huge laying on the white fluffy cloud and appeared as a human, as we seen Him on the ceiling of the Vatican Library. The holographic human image of God was more beautiful that I could imagine. He was taking up a quarter of the Eastern sky. Jesus Christ walked right out of God's heart in the sky. He was holding up a Baby in His holy hands. The baby was wrapped in a simple sturdy cotton towel and as he turned Him toward us, we could clearly see that it was BES, the African Creator Baby god of the Egyptians. Christ held the baby up high in His hands for everybody on Earth to see the wonder. The three wisemen, Gaspar, Melchior and Balthazar looked up to the sky from Earth and they knew the Conception of the Christ was decided in the Heart of God. They looked at each other and smiled. They had 9 months to prepare the gifts and to get the camels and to travel to Bethlehem. All they had to do is to follow the Red Cloud as it moved slowly from East to West in the sky. They knew that when the Celestial Virgin loses her water toward the end of September 2022, the large tsunamis will not let them travel easy. After that they would not be able to travel at all. The 3 ½ years of the Anti-Christ would then begin.

God looked at the Bes Baby. It was so much heat associated with the little Brown Dwarf that the Creator decided to send His Son, Jesus Christ down to Earth as the Holy Baby - as humans could not bear the intense heat Bes put out. He chose Christ to come down and tell the Sacred Celestial Story to those humans that would listen. A godly spark flew out of Bes, and it went into Christ body. God anointed Jesus Christ to be the Messenger of the Cosmic Secret that needed to be told. The Father – God reached out and touched the forehead of His daughter, the Milky Way Celestial Virgin. That is where the Immaculate Conception was born. Then He touched His Heart from where His Son was born. The Father, the Son and the Holy Spirit all came through the body of the Celestial Virgin, the part of the Milky Way God designated to be the sacred birthplace. The Three Wise Men were mesmerized staring at the sky and understanding the gift of God's Creation. Gaspar, the King of the White Men made the sign of the Cross on his body. The Father, the Son, and the Holy Spirit. 'Will the people understand the elaborate Cosmic Creation the three of us just witnessed' – he was thinking it in his mind. He looked at the sky and seen the star constellation Camelopardalis.

"Let us pack up our Camels for the road and honor the Baby with gifts." – Gaspar told the others.

King Gaspar's name was derived from the ancient Hindu name of the first king of Ceylon, Sri Lanka the island in the south part of India. Apparently, according to Hindu creation mythology, it was King Kashi Apa (Turtle Father) who founded the first capital of the island we know as Colombo. Kash the 'Turtle' is not alone in the name of (Kas-par) as the 'par' part means 'pair'. Thus, Kaspar (Gaspar / Casper / Jasper, etc.) meant the 'TURTLE PAIR'. Why would a 'turtle pair' be the founder of the first city after a catastrophic event? – one would wonder. The explanation is very simple. As the North American continent stands for the 'Turtle Island' in the mind of the Native Americans, the other 'turtle' of the pair would be a tectonic plate under the Pacific Ocean. When one of the turtles of the pair would subduct under the other – in response to the Orion Nebula black hole eruption, which would then cause the huge earthquake and the tsunami. Now, suddenly it would make perfect sense to tie the wiseman Gaspar / Kaspar – the 'turtle pair' of the Orion Nebula black hole. Has a Hindu King with the name of Kashi Apa ever existed in flesh? – likely not, but the creation mythology made the concept famous and the three wisemen, the three belt stars or even the three sword stars of Orion made it even to the Bible. Nimrod, the Giant Hunter has revealed the secret of his scientific strength.

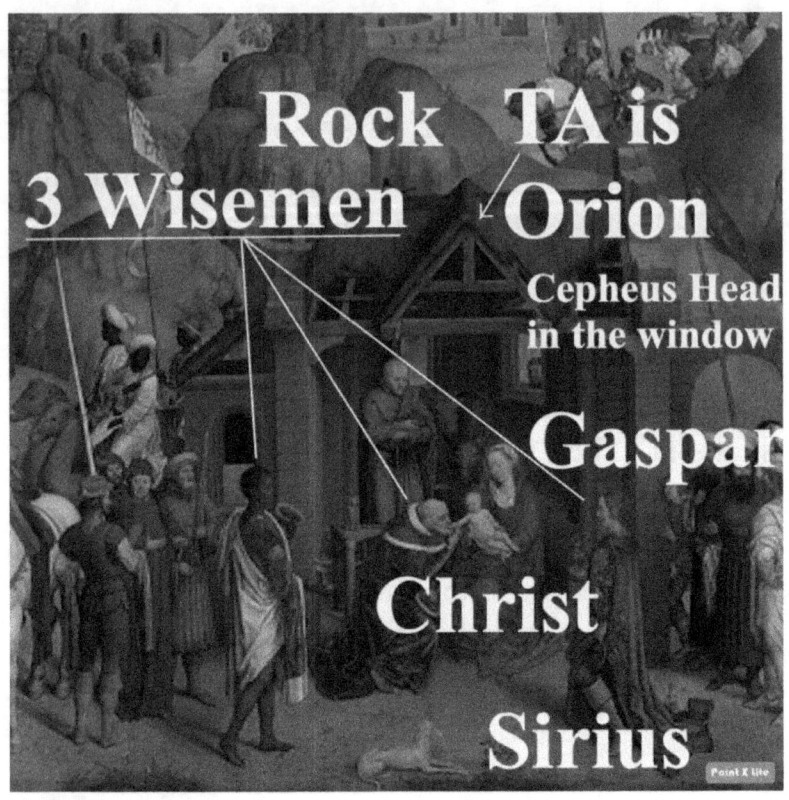

So, was there ever three wisemen, a founding king of the capital Colombo of Sri Lanka – Ceylon, is difficult to determine, but is there an astronomical teaching in these creation stories? – we do not know. We see the scientific teachings, but it is much more difficult to ascertain that there were actual people behind these tales. Here in the Edge of the Atmosphere, we were not too keen on flesh and bone realities as we did not have our own bodies. Everything seemed to be a teaching of the Spirit.

"The Orion Nebula erupted on this Christmas Day of 2021 thus we are obligated to reach the Holy Land by the second half of September 2022, by Rosh Hashanah. It will begin a Cosmic New Year, not only for our Jewish brothers, but for everybody on the face of the Earth. We, the Three Kings represent Astronomy and the varied population of the Earth. I am white, you are black, and he is a middle-Easterner. We are all the people." – Gaspar explained to the other two astronomer kings. "We go on a long journey to honor the Bes, to honor God, and to honor the Holy Spirit who will be incarnated to Earth again. To the Christians it will be the Second Coming of Christ and for the other nations we honor their given names and believes." – Gaspar cheered up the others. They began their preparations for the long journey.

Eva and I looked at the Three Wisemen with overflowing joy, bringing Astronomy into the religious picture. There is hope that the people around the world will understand that the 'Teaching of the Christ and the Cross' involved all the nations around the world. It was the beginning of the re-Birth of Bes, which effected every living creature on Earth. It was the Gift of God of reestablishing the Holy Magnetic Field around the Globe, se we can all live on this magnificent planet. Most of us will die soon and a few live to repopulate the Earth.

"Jesus Christ!" – I sighed out loud.

"I am here my son." – Christ reappeared next to us.

"I don't think I can do this." – I blurted it out.

"Do what?" – Jesus Christ wondered.

"I cannot go house to house to teach this. I cannot tell people of all the bad things that will happen on Earth due to this … event … the birth." - I cried.

"Then who will?" – Christ looked at me with wondering eyes. There was no judgement in His stare. He looked over to Eva who had her eyes fixed on the floor in front of us.

"Nobody would believe us." – Eva pleaded with the Lord. "Nobody!"

"A lot of them will be called on by me, but few will answer. I know that." – Christ stated it. - "It might not even happen if people change their mind and seek the truth and righteousness." – He claimed. Christ waited to see our responses, but we were too paralyzed to even show emotions. Christ continued.

"The destruction happens to the masses because they don't listen, they don't want to know the truth. They go to church, synagogues, or any houses of prayers where most of them ask for health, money, good luck, long life – but they are not asking for wisdom to know the truth. They do NOT want to know the Truth!" – Christ explained with passion.

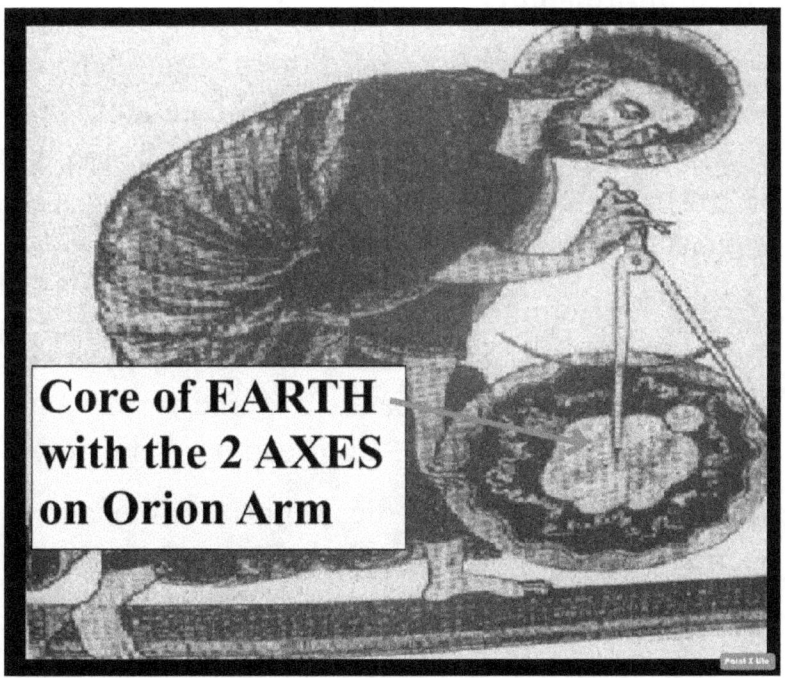

Core of EARTH with the 2 AXES on Orion Arm

"So, let me show you first this picture of me from a French Freemasonic Bible. This was around the time in the 1,300's when the head of the Knight

213

Templars, Brother DeMolay got executed by the French king on Friday the 13th. On my instructions, the Knight Templars painted this picture that would show the CORE OF THE EARTH. The Compass in my hand revealed that our tools hide the knowledge of the Earth's Geo-dynamo. The French King did not like the fact that I was teaching the science of the globe to the people who they finally convinced that the Earth was flat." – Christ informed us.

"So, You, expect me Lord to go and tell the people that the Earth is round with core and if the Red Cloud rises on the East this coming Christmas of 2021 – then the last 14 years to total destruction began." – I asked.

"Yes, the Return of the Destroyer happens every about 110 generations of about 52 years, as the Kolbrin Bible states on pages 234 and further on." – Christ stated it calmly. "You read it for me now."

Jesus Christ produced the Kolbrin Bible and it opened on page 234 for me to read.

"Read!" – Christ instructed me.

FROM THE KOLBRIN BIBLE

"Chapter Three – The Destroyer – Part 1

MAN:3:1   Men forget the days of the Destroyer. Only the wise know where it went and that it will return in its appointed hour.

MAN:3:2   It raged across the Heavens in the days of wrath, and this was its likeness. It was as a billowing cloud of smoke enwrapped in a ruddy glow, not distinguishable in joint or limb. Its mouth was an abyss from which came flame, smoke, and hot cinders.

MAN:3:3. When ages pass, certain laws operate upon the stars in the Heavens. Their ways change; there is movement and restlessness, they are no longer constant and a <u>GREAT LIGHT APPEARS REDLY IN THE SKIES.</u>

MAN:3:4   When blood drops upon the Earth, the Destroyer will appear, and mountains will open up and belch forth fire and ashes. Trees will be destroyed and all living things engulfed. Waters will be swallowed up by the land, and the seas will boil.

MAN:3:5 The Heavens will burn brightly and REDLY; there will be a copper hue over the face of the land, 'followed by a day of darkness'. A new moon will appear and break up and fall.

MAN:3:6. The people will scatter in madness. They will hear the trumpet and battle cry of the Destroyer and will seek refuge within dens in the

Earth. Terror will eat away their hearts, and their courage will flow from them like water from a broken pitcher. They will be eaten up in the flames of wrath and consumed by the breath of the Destroyer."

"Jesus Christ, this is a true horror story! Should I read some more, or we heard enough about the coming of the Destroyer?" – I asked the Lord.

"Read on brave heart." – J. C. asked me.

"Okay, I will read it, but I don't have to believe it or embrace it, right?" – I turned to the Lord.

"This is the Truth on this narrow gate. Read on." – Christ instructed me kindly. I looked back to the pages and started to read again.

"MAN:3:7. Thus it was in the Days of Heavenly Wrath, which have gone, and thus it will be in the Days of the Doom when it comes again. The times of its coming and going are <u>KNOWN UNTO THE WISE.</u> These are the signs and times which shall precede the Destroyer's return: <u>A HUNDRED AND TEN GENERATIONS SHALL PASS INTO THE WEST,</u> and nations will rise and fall. Men will fly in the air as birds and swim in the seas as fishes. Men will talk peace one with

another; hypocrisy and deceit shall have their day. Women will be as men and men as women; passion will be a plaything of man."

"If it is written down this exact then how come people will not prepare for it?" – I asked the Lord.

"Human mind and imagination are not prepared to accept such a level of destruction to come naturally. It has to be hidden from them in stories." – J.C. said.

"Then if it is already written in the Kolbrin Bible, then why we have to be the harbingers of the bad news?" – I argued with the Lord.

"There is no bad news. This is the Truth of the Narrow Gate you both selected. Because if you two don't do it truthfully, we have nobody else who reached the clarity of the message to make it available to the masses." – Christ remained calm and persistent.

I looked over to Eva. She shrugged her shoulders.

"We might look stupid, but if we complete the training, we will live, right?" – She asked me and then turned her attention to the Lord.

"At this point, the time is limited." – Christ looked down to Earth where our almost lifeless bodies were already teetering on the brink of carnal extinction. We did not know what our Lord has seen, but for the look in His eyes, there were concerns for our safety. We did not understand the seriousness of it.

"We signed up to do this, … so might as well go all the way and complete the training." – my wife offered.

"Yes, that is the honorable thing to do." – I agreed, not even knowing that our life was in the balance.

"Listen, I cannot look ahead for you and tell you that everything will be alright. I am not allowed to tell your future on the physical plane. I can only take you both back to the time - when as spirits you decided to go down to Earth and take on this assignment." – Jesus Christ was lecturing us.

"Wait, … I don't fully understand what you are saying J.C. … would you please explain. I already decided I am going to do this job, … but I don't remember signing up for this before I was born. Is that what You are referring to?" – Eva asked.

"Here, let me take both of you back to the names, families, circumstances you both chose to remember this event." – Jesus Christ smiled at us. "You both planned it out to be here today."

"So, we decided to do this before we were even conceived? What about others?" – I asked with surprise.

"Everybody came down with predetermined markers and reminders, but most of them did not pay attention. They got caught in the magic, mysteries and miseries of spirits living in a human flesh." – Christ was smiling at us.

"I don't remember wishing that scorpions would burn me up." – Eva retorted.

"No, but you picked a mother whose last name was Elk, to remind you the magic of the Golden Elk of the Magyar creation legend." – J.C. explained to her patiently. "Her first name was Maria to match the Virgin Mary's name in your Hungarian Judeo-Christian culture. You covered the mysteries of re-creation tales in the pre-Christian and the Judeo-Christian teachings. Then your mother named you Eva after the little Jewish girl she baby-sit before your birth - to bring Judaism to your consciousness, not to mention your paternal grandma's influence in this matter. You gathered up Judaism, Christianity, Euro-Asiatic Shamanism, then later Sioux Indian Native American Spirituality. Scientology, Buddhism, … should I continue?" – Christ was smiling as He rattled off the long list.

"Okay, I see your point." – Eva submitted.

"I am not done." – Christ was still smiling.

"Your father's last name Fej-ős, can either mean 'Ancient Head', or more likely 'Milker', such as the Milking of the Milky Way Cow. … I am still not done. You then pick a husband who were born in September, the month of the birth of Bes, from the Virgo Mother. That signifies the Orion Nebula eruption. Certainly, don't forget that you were born in the zodiac sign of the Aries, reminder of the Day of Re-Creation. You and your husband were born exactly 3 ½ years apart as the time frame of the Anti-Christ. Now, your husband picks a last name Gaspar, who is One of the Three Wisemen in the Bible, representing the Belt of Orion. Not only his birth is in the Virgo sign, where the Orion Nebula eruption happened, but his name points to Orion. He researches the Mayan Calendar and the Egyptian creation legends, where Orion is the first station. His grandpa's name is Adam, your name is Eve or Eva, thus you name your publishing company Adam & Eva. Should I say more." – Christ asked theatrically.

"I don't think there is anything more." – Eva laughed.

"You're wrong." – Jesus Christ faked the upset in His disagreement. Eva looked surprised.

"Your father-in-law was born in a small town called 'Ancient Stone'. Next town was called Pet, which is the reminder of the Egyptian sky. This is by the Lake Balaton in Hungary that was named after 'Baal Aton' (Lake Balaton), the last Shamanic druid priest who was killed by the advancing German Christian Army in 997 AD. Now, if you remember the legend of that event. They killed the Magyar Shaman Bal Aton, who cursed the Hungarian people that they will not have spirituality for 1,000 years. What happened one thousand years later?" – J.C. asked.

"I don't know what You are referring to Christ." – Eva admitted.

"Well, in the summer of 1996, exactly 1,000 years after Bal Aton's curse - you, your husband and two other Hungarians from Hungary participated in the Sioux Lakota Sun Dance in Colorado. You represented Jews, Christians, and Shamanic believers in that Native American ceremony. The two girls, your great friends dancing on either side of you were Rhonda, a mainly African American girl and Erlinda, a Hispanic lesbian girl, who brought your husbands attention to John Major Jenkins, the great American author of the Mayan Calendar books. John cried on your shoulder, he told you secrets he would not share with others, ... he called your husband a great Ice Age researchers in his book Galactic Alignment. Should I go on and on to show you that thousands of pieces of secret information were imparted to you both before and after your births to bring you to this juncture." – Jesus Christ was very convincing.

"So, we chose this path." – Eva stated.

"Yes, you did. Your spirits will not rest until you complete your missions, … or you die." – Christ completed His thoughts and appeared unemotional.

"Why did we choose this horrific path?" – I asked.

"The appointed time, need for salvation, helping humanity survive." – Christ stated with calm tone.

"What did we do to deserve this?" – I asked.

"Let us not list all the sins, you had plenty. Up here though no manmade sins exist." – Christ stated.

"Lately you both lived good honorable lives in the last few hundred years. When you signed up for this assignment as one of the few braves, you asked to have your previous human sins forgiven so you can start the next ice age cycle with a clean slate and be there for the family." – J.C. explained. "Initially, after this - only few spirits will be allowed back to Earth. There will be no 8 billion human bodies needing a godly soul."

"So, if I would not do this assignment, … then what would be my punishment on Earth?" – I asked. I was surprised how much of the moral fighting happened on this heavenly side. Good vs. Evil.

"You would observe for Seven Generations, or about 365 years the destructions of your families due to the sins of what you did and the ignorance you displayed. You would not be allowed to return for 7 generations to correct any of the mistakes, but you would be witnessing the fruits of your actions, observing your great grand children going through the miseries they did not deserve, but thanks to you they got to experience." – Jesus Christ explained.

"That is karma, right?" – I asked.

"It is more than karma, since karma only affects you, but when countless other human beings suffer because of your actions, that lives deep scars on your spirit." – Christ was relentless in His teachings.

"It is complicated." – my wife commented.

"It is more than complicated. Look into the eyes of a rooster, a cow, a pig, a gorilla, or a chimpanzee. You see that they have varying degrees of understanding. They have spirits, like us humans, but they cannot express themselves. A cow knows that you or someone else can kill them for food or just for fun, but they cannot escape it. They cannot argue it or reason with us. They eat the grass and wait to be killed for their meat. Do you know if their spirits were once a fallen human spirit that cannot chose to come back as a human, because they killed other humans through so many of their previous lifetimes – without good reasons – that now the God of Nature only allows them back to physical existence as victims. They experience to be the victims of human hunger of killing, so many times that their spirits grow up to feel again. Then hopefully they will be allowed to be humans again and bring back the subconscious memory of senseless dying. Devolution instead of evolution." – J.C. was not the one talking, but as we looked up, it was Sata who imparted this twisted wisdom on us.

"I don't want to come back as a cow." – she said. "One is then locked into a boring green grass mulching machine that has not much control over what happens to them, around them." – Eva said.

"What! You don't like animals?" – Sata was scratching his hairy skin. His mountain goat face was elongated and shinning with intelligence.

"Okay, if God put humans on Earth, then it would make more sense that the animals devolved from humans. It would better explain the animals that are genetically close to humans. Devolution, instead of evolution." – Sata insisted on his twisted reasoning.

"I honestly think that I cannot take on more stressful moments." – I turned to Sata. Behind him now stood Christ who was worried about my declaration.

"How are you doing?" – J.C. turned toward Eva. She was shaking her head indicating that she was not doing well.

"Where are we going from here? I am worried about your personal wellbeing." – J.C. admitted.

"I don't want to experience all the suffering and pain that is coming in the next few years. I don't feel like I have the physical, emotional or even the spiritual fortitude to complete this task." – I sadly admitted.

"It is pretty tough so far." – Eva agreed with me.

"Well, the decision you are making here now is going to effect not just you, but thousands of people who will need you." – Christ explained.

"We feel that the further we go into the future, the weaker we will get. I am afraid that the more I expose myself to these cruel possibilities, the less I can clearly think and be helpful to anybody." – Eva stated.

"I kind of agree …" – I joined in. Eva looked over to me with a soft face appreciating my support.

"You leave me no choice, but to be brutally honest." – Jesus Christ looked over to Sata, who was looking down to the floor in front of him shaking his head in agreement.

"Well, let's go then." – J.C. prepared us for a trip.

"Where are we going?" – Eva asked with surprise.

"We are going to visit you and your family." – J.C. stated. Sata looked worried.

"I like that." – my wife cheered up. Sata was curling up his lips and shaking his head in disagreement. He straightened out and produced a sharp whistle that brought the golden chariot to our vicinity. J.C. and Sata rushed us into the chariot and the four of us took off toward our house. There was nobody driving the chariot, but it seemed to know where we were heading. The closer we descended to our house, we were surprised to see our friends and even family members crowding the lawn on the outside of our place. Two ambulances with sirens and flashing lights were decorating the street.

"What is that circus?" – Eva seemed to get upset fast.

"The ambulances are getting ready to take you away to the hospital." – Christ explained.

"Take me away, … but I am here." – Eva complained loudly.

"Okay, don't worry about it." – Sata jumped in to cool the emotions. "Think of it as one of the potential futures. Not a reality, yet."

"It looks pretty real to me." – Eva pointed at the events unfolding in front of us. Hovering above our house in a UFO like golden chariot, this sudden visit was a chilling experience.

"Why are they taking us to the hospital?" – I finally spoke up seeing myself tied unto a gurney with an EMS person walking next to me and holding the face mask with oxygen on my face.

"You are being taken to the Emergency Department where both of you will be intubated and placed on ventilators. …" – Sata looked up. As evil as we thought he was – this 'devil' seemed to be concerned over our fate.

"Why?" – Eva was surprised. She had a problem with seeing me in two places at the same time. She was concerned about the one that was rolled into the ambulance in a hurry.

"You were sleeping in the bedroom on Christmas Eve with the car exhaust sneaking into the house from the garage. Willy forgot to turn off the Audi when you got home from shopping – since you told him that he needs to go back and still pick up the wreaths you forgot. But then you changed your mind and told him to just leave it and to help you place the red star on the Christmas Tree. You pushed the button and closed the big garage door, but left the connecting door open to the garage since there were still gifts inside the door to be packed away. ... In this possible future, you are both on the brink of dying from carbon monoxide poisoning." – Sata explained with obvious sadness in his voice.

"What do we have to do to prevent this 'possible' ugly future." – Eva asked with some vigor.

"You both have to complete the course in prophecy we signed you up for. You have to complete your tests to understand the potential future of the narrow gate." – Christ explained to us.

"How do you feel about it honey?"- Eva turned toward me. She had an encouraging look on her face.

"I think we should think about it first. We cannot do this. Too much suffering is involved. We only got to the beginning of the gates, and we are already suffering physically and mentally." – I stated.

"All that suffering hopefully will build our characters. You are the one who used to say that wisdom to the kids." – She reminded me. "Seriously, we need to do this." – my wife kept up the encouragement. She looked to the distance where number of holy men talked amongst each other and began to approach us. It seemed like they emerged from the Darkness of the Sixth Hour and were walking through the Fifth Hour displaying the Lake of Fire. They were heading toward us.

"Rabbi Schneerson, the Seventh Rabbi of the Hasidic Chabad Movement, who a number of his followers considered the Moshiach, the Messiah - approached us first singing a beautiful song all the way. He addressed us with outpouring love.

"I perform a special Bar Mitzvah and Bat Mitzvah for the two of you. If you come through these gates and reach the Fourth one, I will teach you the secret of the Four Cups of Wine, and the Four Questions. It will not be your usual cover story, but the cosmic reasoning. - 'Mah Nishtanah?' – What has changed? – What changed in the Fourth Year? Today it falls on the Hebrew

Calendar year 5,786. This is parallel to your 2026 year. That is the year of Re-Creation, the Year of the Axis Shift." The Rebbe explained. We did not fully understand it. He went on.

"That is the year when the tectonic plates rise, just as the Bread rise with the addition of the yeast to the flour. I will show you why we spell the bread Chametz and the unleavened bread Matzah. You will learn that the two pillars that make up the letters there are hiding the knowledge of the Axis Shift." – Rabbi Schneerson was excited beyond belief.

"But Rebbe, the Passover Pesach happened 3,333 years ago when our people gained their freedom from Egyptian slavery." – Eva felt confused.

"Everything that happened that time with Moses and the Exodus is allegorically built on those cosmic dates 5,786 years ago." – the Rebbe answered. "It does not matter how we became free, but what matters is how G-d recreated the face of the Earth and allowed us to exist another cycle."

"Well, did G-d appear to Moses at Sinai on the 6th day of the 3rd month in the year 2448 from Creation?" – Eva asked the Rebbe. He nodded.

"Our whole Judeo-Christian believe system founded on the fact that G-d appeared to Moses on that day and that initiated the creation of the Torah, the 5 books, the giving of the 10 Commandments and a lot of sacred teachings and mitzvahs important to our faith." – the Rebbe explained.

"Rebbe, since Moses was the adopted brother of the Egyptian pharaoh, did the secret cosmic knowledge of the Egyptians Mystery School influenced his understanding of the Universe?" – Eva kept asking important questions of the Rabbi.

"As the brother to the Pharaoh, Moses was trained by the smartest viziers. He knew all the cosmic secrets that only the royalty had access to. He likely involved the deep cosmic mysteries in his teachings that not only started a new religion away from the Egyptians, but his laws gave a framework to a Jewish Nation how to be a good person. It is natural that he employed a lot of his knowledge of the Egyptian Mystery School Teachings, so he can be hiding important cosmic enigmas amongst the laws and the prayers." The Rebbe concluded.

Another spirit, Hindu this time approached us from beyond and the Rebbe took a break in the red cloud.

"I will teach you the astronomical symbolism of the Fourth Year if you make it that far in your journey. I have the sacred depiction of the dancing gods and goddesses who will unlock the astronomical and cosmological knowledge of the secrets you need to learn. I will show you a picture where the god/goddess both representing the Orion and the Cygnus Beehive of March 26. Those two events are tied together." – Mahendra explained.

"There is no way a normal human can decipher the cosmic secrets out of a dancing Hindu goddess." – I complained to Mahendra.

"You have read the Hindu Myths from the Penguin Classics, the Rig Veda, the Mahabharata. So, look at this picture in details." – Mahendra asked. "With the knowledge you two already gathered from others, some of the Hindu pictures will make sense. Always think Astronomy and Cosmology."

"The dancing goddess does look like Orion with the Sword and the Shield, but in her hands are the iron rods symbolizing the two axes of the Earth. Thus, the Star of David – or the Beehive goes all the way back to India?" – I asked the obvious question.

Mahendra, the wise old Hindu avatar smiled and shook his head sideways. That meant 'yes', I guess.

"I will not give away all the secrets until you two make it to the Fourth station." – the Hindu sage said.

"Don't be so hard on them Mahendra." – the Rebbe reappeared next to the Hindu man. "They will have to know why the Sun was created on the Fourth day of Creation. They will have to know when to sing the Birkat HaChama. Every 28 years when the date falls on Tuesday, the fourth day after the Sabbath Saturday – the next morning on Wednesday the song is sang. So far it happened 206 times since Creation. The last time it happened was on April 8, 2009. On the Julian Calendar it would be March 26th. Now, add 18 years to that and we get to 2027 … or should it be falling on 2026? Well, we should never know if you quit the prophecy school." – Rabbi Schneerson looked up with an examining stare. "I am not the messiah, I told them down there. The messiah is a concept that derives from the 'birth' MOS." – the Rebbe disappeared in the cloud then reappeared again as if he went to bring some additional information from G-d.

"The 'clouds of glory' at Sukkot." – Rebbe smiled.

"Rebbe, the MOS and MES words for 'birth' from the Egyptians is interesting, The Egyptian 'KA' and the Hebrew 'CHA', that is LIFE are important clues, aren't they?" – Eva wanted to get as much information from this holy man as she could.

The Egyptian 'KA' symbol

"Okay. Here is the Egyptian 'KA' life symbol. It supposedly should represent the 'Core of the Earth' as the 'Heart'." – the Rebbe explained. "… and the ARMS are the TWO AXES of the Earth. When the two arms are shown parallel then they mean that the Axis Shift happened."

"Well, that is not easily understandable." – my wife concluded.

"I agree. But understand that the rabbis and the viziers working together tried to create an alphabet in both languages that represented the cosmic secrets. The center Heart was the Earth, the two arms were the two biblical pillars, which are the Magnetic North and the Polar North. The two arms parallel is when the axis shift happened. The viziers working with the Roman letter 'K' - built into the Earth Geo-dynamo – turning the letter 'K' into the letter 'R' to show that there was an axis shift accomplishes the same secret. The 'KA" symbol turned around gave us our 'CHA' ('Ka') for 'life'. La CHAim. Then now you will understand the significance of the spelling of the Hebrew 'bread' to 'unleavened bread'. But for that you will have to speak Hebrew. The main message is that the axis shifts every 5,786 years – which is coming up in 2026 – takes lives away and gives new life to a new cycle and a new humanity.

Hopefully, this time we humans will do better." – the Rebbe acclaimed.

"What about the other names such as King David." – Eva insisted. David was one of her favorites.

"I will show you the combined wisdom of the name DWD – that is the Hebrew King DaWooD, that is David and the Egyptian name TWT, that is King Tut." – the Rebbe was a born teacher.

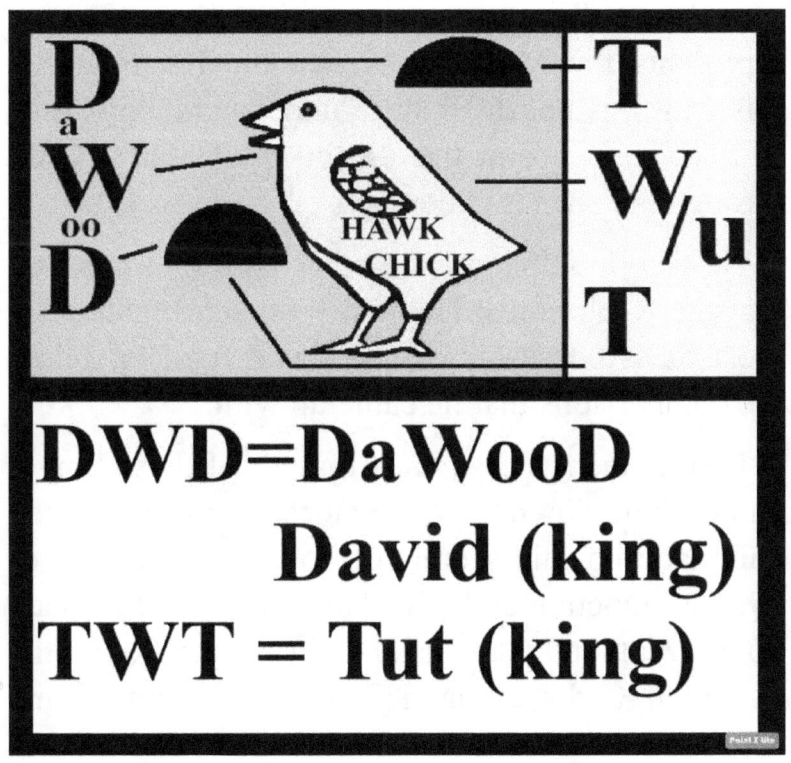

DWD=DaWooD
David (king)
TWT = Tut (king)

"Here you have the Egyptian hieroglyphic spelling of King Tut. The half circle letter represents the upper part of the Earth and thereby represents the two axes of the Earth. The Egyptian letter 'T' turns into the Hebrew letter 'D', or you can think the other way that the Hebrew letter D turned into the Egyptian T. Then in the middle you have the Hawk Chick – the little Prince from Horus, the Magnetic North – that is the Egyptian 'U/W/O', the Hebrew 'W', and the Sumerian Magyar 'Ő'." – the Rebbe stated with eternal confidence. "Furthermore, since the HAWK chick represents the Magnetic North, the IRON ROD, this way it is not difficult to understand why Jesus Christ came from the 'Root of David'. Only through the stars it makes sense,"

We were looking at each other with Eva thinking that the Rebbe must have an IQ much higher than most of us possess, because it was hard to follow the comparisons that he came up with.

"Rebbe, then you suggest that all of these kingly names boil down to the names of the stars, the enigmatic cosmic secrets of how the Earth's geo-dynamo function and what happens when the black holes erupt, and they shake and shift the axis of the Earth on G-d's demand?" – I asked with some surprise in my voice.

"Most people cannot deal with the Truth, so we entertain them elaborate human stories that hides these cosmic secrets, down to the shape of the letters. But, since you are in the Hall of Truth and you picked the possible worst-case scenario for the climate change, I can be frank with you." – the Rebbe explained.

"I don't understand why most people cannot learn how Nature works?" – I insisted.

"Think of it this way. A human body is the whole Universe. Every cell is important in the human body, but still a brain cell could not communicate with a skin cell on a complex subject. The skin cell thinks we are here on Earth to protect the body from heat, cold, virus, bacteria, insults. The brain cell is trying to explain that there is more to creation, … but when you cut yourself and the skin does not heal then the body dies with the smart brain in it. Some of us are 'brain cells' with a spiritual purpose and we can communicate with each other just fine, but others would not understand us. They still have very important functions to perform. The complexities of the cosmic secrets and how they are hidden in the writings and the oral stories are not for them to know." – the Rebbe finished and disappeared in the Red Cloud of Glory.

A huge holographic image of a whale appeared in the sky. He opened his mouth and Jonah walked out of the belly of the biblical whale. A few drops of water sprinkled of his cloths. He turned around and with a quick movement of his arm showed the whale that he can disappear now, which he did.

"I wanted to teach you two the secret of the Cosmic Whale, but I can only do it if you stay in the training." – Jonah appeared in front of us. "The MES / MOS birth sign of the Egyptians gave the name Moshe, that you know as Moses and the name Moshiach the Hebrew Messiah. I do not even want to tell you that RaMOS, RaMESses, TutMos, your Magyar name Vil-MOS, the Queen E-MES-e, and her son Prince Ál-MOS (Amos) all were made with the Egyptian 'BIRTH' sign. It comes from the COSMIC WHALE, but you will not know the full implication if you quit the journey." – Jonah explained.

"How is that Cosmic Whale tied to the BIRTH?" – I asked. My voice was weak, and I felt mentally and physically exhausted and I knew that I was dying. I was not dead, yet. I was close to it.

"When you look at that the Cosmic Whale, it is constructed out of the GALACTIC PLANE, SOLAR PLANE and the EQUATOR. If you know how these three planes tie into the Geo-dynamo then you will start understanding what we have been trying to teach you. The Cosmic Whale is one of the big secrets. Do you get it now?" – Jonah asked.

"Not entirely." – I was too weak to think.

"Honey, try a little harder. You cannot die on me now, ... or I will kill you." – Eva was truly mad.

"I will try." – I murmured. Eva shook her head.

Jonah raised his arms to get our attention.

"I will show you the cosmic secret of the THREE LINES the make up the Egyptian BIRTH hieroglyphic symbol. Let me show it to you. The Sumerian Magyars, your ancestors went down to Egypt and made this hieroglyphic system. Because so many words are derived from your language, it is almost impossible to find another pair of seekers who could help us explain these enigmas. Pay attention, the GALACTIC PLANE, the SOLAR PLANE, and the EARTH'S EQUATOR make up these lines. The two important black holes Cygnus and Orion, and the Sun are positioned on these three lines. That is why the viziers chose the MOS / MES Birth symbol. This is where BES birth come from, and this is what most holy men, Moses, Christ, and others recorded down with their own examples – albeit hiding the real cosmic truth about it. Regular human mind is not equipped to understand the powers the move Earth, the Sun, the Galaxy. If we do not package the cosmic teachings into made up human history that can be later discovered, then the celestial wisdom disappears for humanity. If you two will stay in the prophet school, then I promise you to teach the Cosmic Whale to you in such details that very few people understand. You will have to earn the right to know these deep secrets that only a few humans understand. I will not go into fine details until then." – Jonah sounded stern.

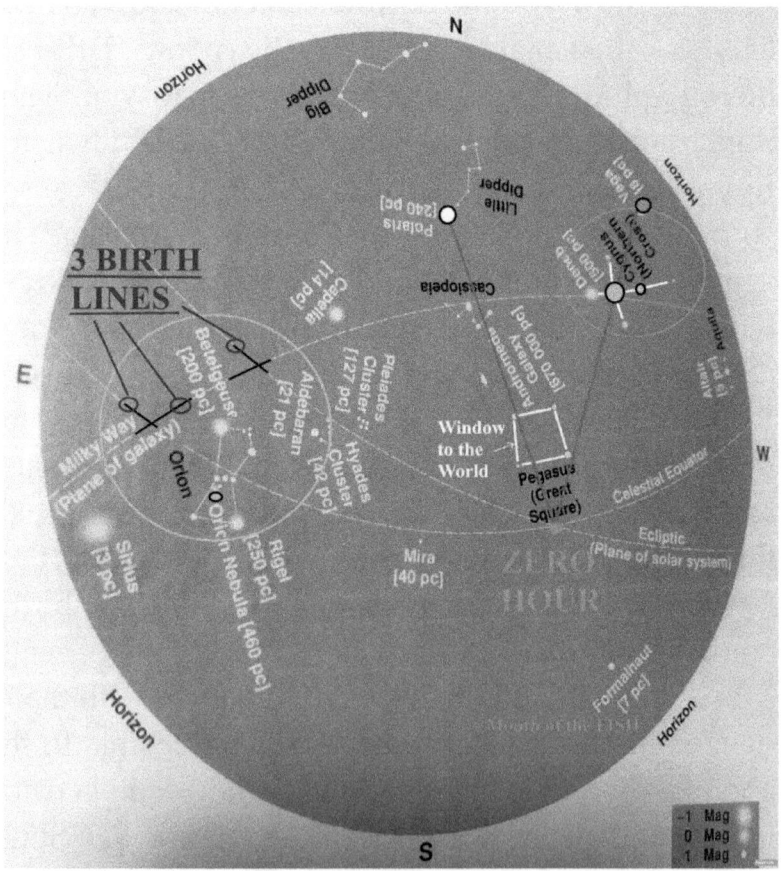

"What is scary that the Hindus, Sumerians, Egyptians, the Hebrews and a few other civilizations used the same advanced star knowledge." – Eva exclaimed. Jonah nodded.

"There are two black holes on this picture. One is in the Urinary Bladder of the Whale. In secret circles that is called 'Vesica Piscis'. If you stay alive in the Hall of Truth, these knowledges will be yours. Both of you will be well versed in secret cosmic knowledge that nobody on earth knows officially. You'll deliver the news." – Jonah explained.

"If I can help show you the Hindu version of this Cosmic Whale, I hope it will help you to get back on the journey." – Mahendra reappeared in the picture. "Here is the Hindu Cosmic Whale."

"If you look at that picture, it is made in the image of the Astronomical Cosmic Whale. At the rudder is the Orion Nebula black hole. Most importantly though in the BLOWHOLE of the Whale is a horn pillar, which is tied to the neck of the Black Swan. That identifies the blow hole as the CYGNUS X-3 black hole whose eruption on March 26th 5,786 years ago caused the Axis Shift." – Mahendra explained.

"Then the staff that is stuck in the blow hole of the Cosmic Whale represents the Magnetic North." – Eva cleverly explained. "The Living Water of the Galaxy and the Universe in the Magnetic North."

"I am glad sister that you woke up out of your beauty sleep." – Cleopatra appeared on the scene to coax Eva back into the game. The male gurus politely pulled back into the veil.

"I was never into whales. Hard to pat them, they are too big." – Eva stated with a straight face. "Not even your pregnant hippopotamus stirs up my mood." – she smiled as she was joking with Cleopatra.

"Huh, don't tell me. What about the time when you were standing in the Crystal River in Florida patting the belly of a pregnant manatee? You don't think I had something to do with that teaching moment?" – Cleopatra was laughing at my wife out loud.

"Look at that picture. You are in the water and under the surface of the river is a pregnant manatee who lets you just pat her." – Cleopatra was very proud next to Queen Emese that they did something to awaken Eva. "You understand that when something unusual happens it is divine intervention to raise your awareness."

"Wow, I can see it!" – an animated Queen Emese chirped into the discussion. "You look great! Actually – I look great. Now I can see the resemblance to my own face. You are me. That is just so amazing." – the Queen was in a good mood.

"Maybe Willy is right. I go on vacation to Florida to enjoy myself and the two of you sending me pregnant manatees to have a clue about something that I have no clue about. I am kind of tired. This journey in the Hall of Truth seems much more difficult that I am prepared to commit." – Eva was sounding exhausted.

"Eva, you who are me, - listen to me. It was my spirit who went into that manatee in Florida on your vacation. I could not get a pregnant hippopotamus from the Nile, as Cleopatra suggested." The Queen was happy cracking polite jokes. She turned her voice serious.

"I hope you understand that it was my spirit driving the manatee to give you a sense of vision about the cosmic meaning of the Egyptian pregnant hippopotamus. That was the best I could think of. The fact that it was on March 26th totally avoided your attention." – Queen Emese was explaining it to Eva. She was reaching toward her in a manner to pull her up, reenergize her. "You need to complete the journey. I know you think you learnt a lot, but there is so much more to know. Your suffering will be done for humanity. It will be a proper way to finish this whole ice age cycle for all three of us, right Cleopatra? Our sons suffered yours don't have to." – the Magyar Queen and the Egyptian queen stared at Eva with overwhelming love.

"Remember the story of the Magyar Prince Álmos, my son who established the lineage of the kings who ruled Hungary between the years 1,000 and 1,301? Remember how I had the HAWK Horus flew over my tent when I realized that I was pregnant with my son from the Holy Spirit?" – Emese looked over to Eva who nodded in agreement. "Those were cosmic teaching that we Sumerian Magyars and the Egyptians recorded down for this age. Whose is going to do the same for this coming New Age? There are no candidates who even come close to how far you progressed so far. So, you can give in and not take on the task. Only humanity will suffer on the physical level, but here in spirit - we will always be good." Queen Emese completed her pep talk.

8.

Infinity

"Is he still stable on the machine? – my beautiful daughter Rubina asked with a stern voice not to show weakness. Her voice crackled a little bit, but at least she was able to hold back the crying. "It's been 7 days. Do we have to make the decision, or we have some more time left?" Our daughter Rubina Xenia was staring at the doctor in the ICU.

"Let's step out of the ICU and we can talk a little bit more freely." – Dr. Kelly suggested.

"What's going on with your Dad Babe?" – Taylor, my daughter's fiancé sounded concerned. His great character made him an instant star in our family.

"Well, the doctor is saying that they don't know why he is still relying on the ventilator, because the carbon monoxide is long out of his system. He is in a coma and thus ventilator dependent without a good explanation. If he stays like this, they either want us to take him off the machine and he can die or have them do a tracheostomy and keep him on the machine. Then send him to the long-term acute care hospital. Is this correct Dr. Kelly?" – Rubina turned to the slim, tall, and handsome doctor.

"That's right. The LTAC would be his best bet to come out of this. I wish I knew why he is requiring high PEEP and then we cannot wean him off the machine because he desaturates. Same with your mom. Their covid's are negative and there is no pneumonia. I don't get it." – Dr. Kelly explained. His phone went off and it seemed like they wanted him back in the ICU. He raised his hands in an apology and walked back to the ICU swiftly. Makayla, the pretty blond ICU nurse came out to explain to Austin and the rest of them what was happening inside. She was calm, thorough with her explanations, but seemed concerned. Apparently, there was more PEEP needed to have the ventilator provide better lung support.

"What are we going to do?" – our son Austin turned to Rubina and Taylor. He might have been nervous, but he did not show it.

"I am going to ask them for one more day before we decide on the tracheostomy. Both for him and mom." – Rubina stated with confidence.

"That is a good idea for now." – Austin agreed. Taylor was nodding his head. One could tell that at this point they just wanted to have a little bit more time to make the right decisions.

"I still don't understand how they left the car running in the garage Christmas Eve with the connecting door open to the house. I doubt they wanted to commit suicide." – Austin stated.

"I've been going through these senseless scenarios for days now. I can't sleep but a few hours. You guys have to help me make the right decision by the morning." – Rubina pleaded with the boys.

"You see what you are putting your family through?" – Jesus Christ was asking the both of us. He took us down to the hospital in spirit to see what was happening. It was a sad picture.

"We are not really sick, right? We are not in the hospital … because we are here talking to you? Right, … being on the machine, this is just a possible future?" – I was asking J.C. in a hurried manner. I was very nervous about this scenario.

"You are sick, and you can die. Your mind is sick, fighting your spirit to make the right choice. It is in turmoil. That is the truth. The explanation may not make sense to you, but this is how things are unfolding. Getting back on the journey of the Narrow Gate and completing your tasks will be the only thing that can heal you." – J.C. was not making it easy on us.

"Okay, let's do it then for our children and future grandkids." – I turned to Eva after I seen the worried faces of our children earlier. "We have gone through some hard things in the past, one more run at it will not kill us. Right?" – I turned to my wife for encouragement. I did not choose my words carefully.

"We have always done the hard stuff together and we always succeeded. It will be no different now." – Eva agreed with me.

"Let's get back on the road." – my voice felt much stronger. Christ was smiling with joy.

"Okay love." – Eva's agreement was reassuring.

As soon as we agreed to do the journey in the Hall of Truth, we were transported back to the suffering we witnessed. It was the second half of September when usually the Jewish people start thinking about the New Year, Rosh Hashanah when we arrived at the top of a smaller mountain in California. We felt a powerful earthquake and seen buildings collapsing. As we looked down to the distance on the West, there was a wall of white water approaching us from the Pacific Ocean. The West Wall! This was a large tsunami, much larger than the Indonesian event was on December 26th, 2004. Wooden houses were floating on their sides and debris littered the ocean water. Cows, horses, dogs, and even other wild animals were rolling in the approaching water. People were caught up in the waves and they were swimming for their lives.

Trees were floating in the water with large trees that were ripped out of the ground. The roots of the trees were telling about a great tragedy. It occurred to me that the Indonesian tsunami of 2004 was apparently due to a black hole eruption that happened 14 hours prior, but 44,600 light years away from our solar system. This was reported by Dr. Paul La Violette, an independent astrophysicist. If an eruption from that far away could cause the Indonesian tsunami, then it made sense that this Orion Nebula black hole eruption from 1,400 light years away caused a much larger earthquake and tsunami. The devastation was so horrific that all we could do is cry and pray for the people who were fighting for their lives. Both Eva and I walked under the muddy water and witnessed the devastation firsthand with death all around us. We walked out of the water and death were looking at us from all direction. There are billions of planets and only one we know for sure has human life. 'Why is this senseless destruction?' - Eva and I were discussing the subject as we walked out of the area of death?

"You think the pandemic killed a lot of people, what do you think about life and death of the masses now?" – Christ asked us. "No vaccine for this."

"I feel like throwing up." – Eva complained.

"This is terrible." – I admitted. "What else we need to experience to be done with this? Will it get worse, will the trees turn to ashes, the sky explodes and the oceans boil?" – I asked J.C. hurriedly.

"This next station, I will give you a break – I fly you over from the sky for you to inspect. I sense that the physical experience on Earth might kill you." – J.C. admitted. "After that I will provide you with a break to recoup. I will let you talk to some people to see if you pass the pre-test. Then once you gained some experience, I will bring you back to take your real tests. Back on Earth – after this experience – you will have a much harder time to live the human life. I am just warning you to go slow and feel out your subjects." – Jesus Christ advised us.

"Do you feel secure?" – the two angels who scooped us up from above asked us.

"Yes." Came the answers. Both of us felt secure under the protections of the angels who lifted us up and took us out to the sky from where we could look down and witness the action. Soon we heard a large earthquake then another one. A total of four earthquakes shook the globe within days or weeks, - we could not tell the passing time as everything seemed to be observed as if we were fast forwarding the events. Each of the enormous earthquakes caused the Pacific tectonic plate to subduct under the North American tectonic plate. We have seen the Rocky Mountains lifted a total of 6,400 feet while exactly 180 degrees away on the other side of the globe the Himalayas were sinking. The whole Earth was moving, and the surface was rippling up. It felt like Nature was using a heavy wooden roller from the West to make a bread out of our globe. The mountains and the islands all moved out of their places. The volcanoes intensified and lava was pouring out of them. The underwater volcanoes erupted and turned the oceans red colored. The hydrocarbon gas bubbles, looking like the winged disks with open gaping mouths were breathing toxic fire on Earth. The few people who were bravely stupid to be outside were praying and shouting toward the burning sky. 'Lord, burning Face of God – save us from the Destroyer'. Skin burns, like the Boil of Egypt began to develop on their skins. The few smart people who had deep caves dug in the sides of the mountains were yelling at their relatives to come into the safety, but people were mad and did not listen. They were determined to fight this satanic force with the strong faith in a good God. The forests were burning all around them, everything burnt to ashes and by the time they could retreat to the safety of the deep caves, they burnt injuries were fatal. There was no separating the unblemished humans from the injured ones. It did not take long before rotting death carcasses attracted the billions of flies. We looked up in the sky at it was March 26th. The celestial birth of the Lamb of God brought fiery destruction. This was the first time we understood the symbolism of the Astronomy of the Aries pascal lamb and why she had the Musca Fly sitting on her far side.

Soon the oceans and the lakes began to boil and there were no safe places on our planet to comfortably survive these events. Only the cave dwellers more than 10 stories underground survived. A new humanity of cavemen began.

"Now, I understand why the Bible warned us to dig ourselves into the sides of the mountains when we see the 'Face of God'." I turned to Eva, who was just shaking her head in disbelief. "Remember Cutie – Destruction of Humanity chapter in the book by Wallis Budge titled the Legends of the Egyptian Gods, where the viziers were told to place the Winged Disc shape above the main gates on all the temples? So, this hydrocarbon bubbles are the winged discs, the Face of an angry God. Now I understand why there is the Winged Disc above the bust of George Washington inside the Washington Monument and above the library door of Pope Gregorius XVI in the Vatican." – I was telling Eva who was watching the destruction with disbelief.

"So, that is the same reminder to the Destruction of Humanity by the Winged Disc motto on the cars, bikes, airplanes, such as Bentley, Mini Morris, Harley and hundreds of others?" – She seemingly asked but I saw on her face that she already knew the answer to her question. We turned our attention back to Earth from the safety of the angels carrying us high in the sky.

The winged disc shaped burning hydrocarbon bubbles that hovered in the sky as evil auroras, constantly changing their ugly shapes - pretending to be huge hungry celestial gaping mouths with crooked teeth that came to devour humans.

These were the scariest events we have ever experienced. Christ must have told the two angels to fly us high enough above Earth so we would not see the expected human tragedy in full force. We looked in the distance. Both black holes, the Orion Nebula, and the Cygnus X-3, were firing toward Earth and causing immense destruction on our globe. Finally, we have seen two people comically walking on an open area and shielding each other from the rays of the Cygnus X-3 black hole that was pointing at Earth and showering the globe with laser like radiation. The cows and the deer and elk were running away, but soon succumbed to the insane destruction that came out of the Womb of the Milky Way Goddess.

"Here is the Birth of the Spotted Deer." – Nimrod, the Great Hunter lifted the animal high in the sky for us to see. The spotted little Bambi looked gorgeous. All hunting societies were looking at him in awe. Next to him, Jesus Christ lifted a small lamb.

"Here is the Lamb of God." – J.C. proclaimed as he presented the animal toward the watchful eyes of the agricultural folks from the sky.

I was so surprised that somehow - I got loose from the grip of the angel.

"Wow!" – I shouted in fear, but after a few seconds of free floating it became enjoyable. I seen Eva also freefalling ahead of me and heading toward the broken-up Earth. The closer we fell the greener the surface of the globe began to look. In front of our eyes the wounds of the globe began to heal fast.

"Willy, wake up!" – I heard my wife demanding my attention. I did not see her, yet as I was still watching from above the people celebrating. Little kids were playing all over the fields and screaming in joy to be outside and see our beautiful Earth regenerating. The magnetic field had to be much stronger, as every living creature seemed strong and vibrant. In my fall finally I hit the ground, but it was a soft landing. Someone pulled me up in my hospital bed. The endotracheal tube was out my throat.

"Are you up honey? Talk to me." - I heard Eva encouraging me back into reality.

"I'm up." – I mumbled. Someone sat me up higher in the hospital bed. I still could not see as I felt a wet rag wiping my face and a plastic tube stuck deep into my mouth suctioning out excess saliva.

"Cough!" – Jo, the female Respiratory Technician instructed me in a stern voice. I coughed.

"Where am I?" – I asked with surprise in my voice as nothing in the room seemed familiar. Finally, Eva's face started getting into focus. I felt relieved. She will tell me where I am. I coughed again and my throat felt dry and irritated.

"I had such a strange dream." – I told my wife in a crackling voice.

"I know honey." – Eva told me reassuringly and pat my arm. "I will go out now for a few minutes so the kids can come in to say hello, then I will be back to talk. She was sitting back in her wheelchair and the nurse rolled her back into her own room.

Next day we both insisted to be released home and be following up with our Primary Care

Physicians in a few days. We were given a few prescriptions and instructions that we knew we will not follow, regardless we listened to all the warnings they poured on us.

For the next few days, I was just sitting and playing on my computer at home doing research on strange subjects after the kids left. Eva was cooking amazing dishes, something that she is the best at, but we were not even hungry. We sat on the couch holding hands or went for a short walk silently.

I wanted to tell my wife the idiotic crazy dreams I had while being intubated in the hospital, but anytime I tried to bring up the subject I began to cry so violently that no meaningful discussion was going to follow that. She kept holding me close, but she did not ask me 'what's wrong?', which I felt was strange. My job was very understanding allowing me to stay off work for another week to recover.

"Do you need to talk to a psychologist, a medicine man, a rabbi or a priest?" – Eva was asking me with concerned voice after my repeated crying spells. It was not me. I don't cry easily.

"And say what, that I had a scary dream, … and I cry a lot lately?" – I looked at her with a questioning stare. "You think it will help me?"

"It could. Something that will allow you to open and talk about your fears. I can contact David, Calvin, Tom, Bad Hand or any of the medicine men we know and ask for a sweat lodge?" – Eva offered.

"I would love to do a sweat lodge." I suddenly cheered up. "…, but just the two of us. I make the fire and heat the stones and you can run it for us." – I pleaded with her happily.

"Is that a "legal obaghi' plead?" – Eva asked me.

"It is!" – I said with confidence knowing that there is a proper way to ask a medicine woman – albeit officially not a prophet, yet - to perform a sacred ceremony. I ran to bring sage, tobacco, and a rare silver dollar with me. "Maza ska, na chanli chichahu yello. ('I brought You White Metal and tobacco.')" – I said it with awkward Lakota Sioux dialect.

"Ah, you brought me 'chanli', … tobacco. Washte, very good. What do you desire from me? How can I help?" – my wife was taking this seriously.

"I want to have a sweat lodge ceremony. I would like You to run it for us. I need a good sweat, singing, drumming and some hard praying." – I said as I was handing her over a silver dollar and a bundle of sage along with natural tobacco.

261

Eva walked with me to the pile of volcanic rocks by the Sweat Lodge and stopped. She was praying and I stood by her quietly. Finally, she spoke.

"Heat up 26 regular size rocks and two extra large ones. A total of 28 rocks we will use in this ceremony." – She looked up. I did not ask, I figured she will tell me her choice of the number of rocks if it was needed to. "5,786 numerically ads up to 26. 2026 is a special year. Cygnus X-3 turns the Sun in one day for 24 hours and Cygnus X-1 creates the 28 days Moon cycle. 24, 26, 28 - since, I as a female run the Lodge, it will be 28 volcanic rock grandfathers for the female Moon to teach us in there their wisdom. Mitakuye Oyasin – We are All related." – Eva completed her explanation.

She walked away to prepare for the ceremony, and I began to make the sacred fire to heat up the volcanic rocks, which represented the VOLCANIC CORE OF THE EARTH. How strange! I had to learn the science of the Earth's geo-dynamo from the seemingly 'uneducated' Native Americans.

It was sad that we initially looked at the Native Americans as uneducated savages and almost destroyed their cultures that contained important cosmic secrets. In their simplicity of praying to the same Great Spirit or Holy Spirit we pray to, they constructed simple religious tools to remember cosmic science. The sweat lodge ceremony was done in the dome shape tent. The pit that was dug inside the round tent was itself round to represent the core of the Earth. The volcanic rocks piled up in the pit inside then represented the rock core of the Earth inside the globe. Instead of having an elaborate story about the Greek deity Vulcan, who was 'lame' because his legs were the legs of the globe. Vulcan secretly represented the volcanic core of the Earth, but it was not as simple and visual as the Lakota constructed. Our Lakota Sioux people maintained the same concept in a simple sweat lodge sauna structure for the so important knowledge of the geo-dynamo. Water was poured on the volcanic rocks in the darkness of the lodge and the sweating of the people recreated the intense humid heat the Earth experienced every 5,786 years. While Moses face got burned and the Exodus of the Jews were happening through the Red Sea, and Christ was walking through the hot desert for 40 days – this 'inipi' sweat lodge ceremony brought the concept of the changing climate to my consciousness much better than any religious stories. The lame Greek god Vulcan, who was also a blacksmith inside Earth - was a distant second.

My mind was wondering and remembering the stories we learned from our family, from the medicine people we met, from the books we read. By the medicine man Black Elk, there were 7 rights of the Oglala Lakota Sioux Indians. It was brought to them by the White Buffalo Calf Maiden who tumbled and rolled – as the Earth tumbled and rolled during the axis shift – the rare White Buffalo arrived to meet the people to bring them the Sacred Pipe. As I was tending the sacred fire and watched the dancing embers in the sky my mind was busy recalling these stories. It was peaceful sitting by the hissing wood giving off heat. My imaginative mind began to connect the astronomical significance of the White Buffalo Maiden to the Golden Calf of the Jewish people. Then in my wondering mind full of Comparative Mythologies, the Golden Elk became the same star knowledge. There were numerous Bulls of the Sumerian, Hindu, Egyptian, Greek, Roman mythologies that were secretly representing this knowledge that all civilizations and cultures recorded down for us, and almost lost the meaning just right before it became important. I sighed. Just as a priest or a rabbi preparing for a sermon, I had to force my mind to return to the meaning of this approaching sweat lodge ceremony and to pray in preparation.

"The sweat Lodge ceremony called 'Inipi', means 'TO LIVE AGAIN'!" – I remembered out loudly.

It suddenly hit me. 'To Live again' is the 'Re-Birth!'. Just as Christ was teaching with His sacred death and rebirth example.

Suddenly, my mind connected the 3 days Christ was laying, … - dead before His RE-BIRTH inside the CAVE that was to me representing the INSIDE OF THE EARTH. Then there was a STONE that TURNED! Oh my God! The STONE that was blocking the Cave had to be the allegorical STONE inside Mother Earth. The 'turning' then had to represent the turning of the CORE of the Earth into a New Age after the TWO AXES OF THE EARTH UNITED. All of this happened on March 26 almost 5,786 years ago. All of this is connected back into the Legend of the magical GOLDEN ELK, Hebrew GOLDEN CALF, Lakota WHITE BUFFALO and naturally all representing the HEART OF THE TAURUS BULL, THE **PLEIADES**! The biblical passage of the Book of Job from Chapter 9, verses 4-9 reminded me that it is only God who can remove the mountains from their places by the actions of the star constellations ORION, **PLEIADES** and the BEAR.

The sparkling embers from the fire pit heating the sacred volcanic rocks awakened and became more animated. It reminded me to rearrange some of the logs on top of the rocks to slow down the fire. I stirred up the fire that was representing to me the

FIRE OF NIMROD – ORION from the nearest black hole. The same black hole the ancient Mayans called the FURNACE. It all made perfect sense in my mind. I realized that my Lakota ancestors who designed this sacred ceremony - also connected the fire pit as the Orion black hole furnace outside the sweat lodge – to the volcanic rocks inside the sweat lodge, that is inside the Mother Earth. Some sweat lodge doors around the Reservations were facing the West and others were arranged to look toward the East. Our sweat lodge door was properly facing toward the EAST, ORIENTED to the ORIENT where the Furnace of ORION was positioned. This was truly the Mayan Furnace affecting the Core of the Earth. It was magical sitting by the fire at 8,052 feet elevation and meditating over creation stories of the ancients, realizing the magical wisdom they contained.

Thus, this sacred 'inipi' sweat lodge is one of the seven Lakota ways to remember Re-Creation that happens roughly about every 5,786 years. This was the 'Inipi' sweat lodge ceremony 'to live again'. Suddenly, I remembered decades ago in the 90's when we were sitting in a dark basement with windows covered to have a Yuwipi ceremony with Grandpa Bad Hand. My friend and spiritual brother Calvin Standing Bear invited us to participate. In preparation I memorized a Lakota prayer from a tape I was listening to and to the amazement of the natives, I recited that prayer in the dark as if I was a fluent Lakota speaker. The medicine man was surprised. He told me that I will be one of the souls who will help the Lakota people survive into the New Age. As I was thinking, I hoped that this ceremony, my knowledge of the worldwide creation legends and the timing of cosmic events I was given – will be an instrument of the Universal God to make that happen. As I was reminiscing, Eva appeared in the distance bringing her sacred drum with her. She was dressed in an ankle long sweat lodge dress and had a sage crown on her head. She walked humble and proud, but her spirit was soaring high above the tall pine trees surrounding the area where the sweat lodge was strategically located for this sacred ceremony. We both felt that this sweat lodge will provide us with clarity of what's happening to us.

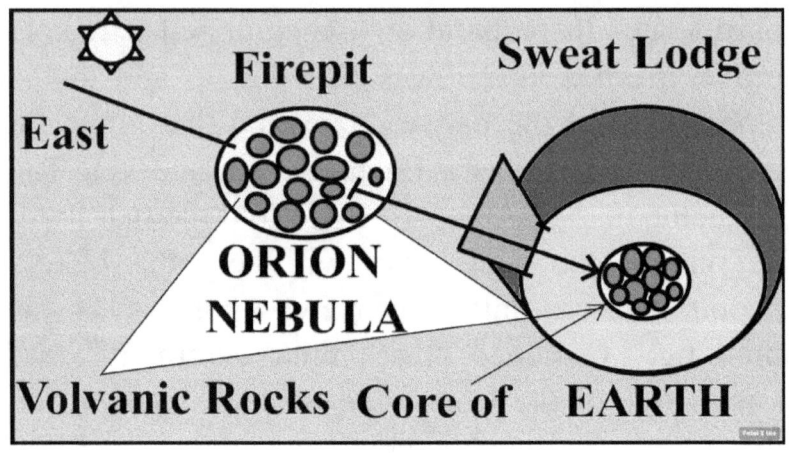

Eva arrived dressed in a long modest traditional ceremonial outfit that reached down to her ankles. At 8,052 feet elevation on our mountain property in northern New Mexico, it was a good dress to wear on a cool day. Although, she is usually not a person who makes her own clothing, she made this dress for herself for the special occasions. My wife looked up with reverence on the snow peaked mountains across from our property. We were in the 'buffalo valley' of our property where hundreds of people were watching the Native American Sun Dance just a few years ago. There were visitors from Italy, France, Switzerland and from all around the US to watch the sun-dancers perform another sacred ceremony of the Sioux Lakota Indians. The white peak across from us that we were staring at was over 12,000 feet tall and most of the year it was covered with snow in the El Alto region. When one dances half naked in the blazing sun for four days in July – not eating or drinking for four days – the site of snow as life giving frozen water gave the dancers some encouragement. The flesh piercing ceremony torn the body away from the sacred Sundance Tree. That was another cosmic teaching.

Standing by the fire and looking at the snow across the mountain top gave us an interesting feeling of opposites. Heat and cold.

"Beautiful." – I stated the obvious. Eva and I were staring at the mountain peak reminiscing over good times. The 12,000 feet tall mountain ridge is called the SANGRE DE CHRISTO, the BLOOD OF CHRIST. How appropriate. We are staring at a mountain ridge called with the sacred name of Christ and His blood. The snow peaked region seemed so close we could almost touch it, but if we tried to walk up there it would take us a day or two. The snow cover that persisted throughout most of the year melted slowly and provided a rich water source underground. The rivers that were running 100 feet below the surface occasionally broke out of the ground in the form of small natural springs. We had one unique natural spring on our land where the bears, elks and the deer would come to quench their thirsts. We even had tracks of a mountain lion in the area on the land.

This was a special land we owned, and we were ready to do some special praying in the sweat lodge. We smudged all around our bodies with the smoke of the sage for purity, and my wife paused at the door of the lodge. She was on all four crouching down. Before she entered - Cutie placed her forehead on the beginning of the entrance to the sacred sweat lodge representing the round globe we live on. She was praying for several minutes with her forehead to the ground and would not enter the Holy of Holies, the symbolic inside of the Earth where the life preserving volcanic stone core was positioned. Then she slowly crawled into the lodge and sat down on the right side of the door where usually the sweat lodge leader would sit. The tarp flap that was made to be the door was curled up on top of the round lodge that was not bigger than a Volkswagen 'bug' car. This time this was our 'vehicle' to travel to the spirit world with our questions and prayers. I was waiting outside for her to give me the sign to start bringing in the hot sizzling volcanic stones to the lodge. The dark gray volcanic stones were shinning orange yellow inside and emitted a lot of heat. I loved to look at the hot rocks in the fire pit. The heat was so intense it burned my face. I thought of Moses with the burning bush and the burning of his face. The stories were from different times all meaning one event.

"Washte, start bringing the grandfathers in." – Eva instructed me referring to the hot volcanic stones. "First bring three then pause a little and bring me four more to add up to seven, the rests after that." – She asked me. I scooped up the first stone carefully with a pitchfork, being careful not to drop it on the ground. It was not allowed to let the stones touch the soil outside the lodge, as they were sacred and only belonged to the inside of the lodge, inside Mother Earth.

"Pffff!" - I blew on the rock with a big blow from the lungs to get rid of sooth and impurities before I transport them to the door. The rocks had to be pure.

"Mitakuye Oyasin ('We are all related')" – I stated my Lakota 'amen' as I placed the pitchfork inside the door of the lodge with a large burning volcanic rock on top. This was the first time the pitchfork was allowed to be resting on the ground, since now we were inside the Holy of Holies. Iron was okay, as it was part of the core of the Earth. Cutie first touched the rock with her sage bundle to bless it. She quietly mumbled a prayer to bless the rock. Then Eva opened her leather medicine pouch and sprinkled some of the dry cedar leaves on the rock and they sizzled and gave off some nice aroma. I remembered that the cedar was from the cypress family. The sweat aroma, the burnt offering brought a sense of biblical importance to this action.

"Next!" – Eva awakened me from my meditative state. I went and carefully scooped up another volcanic rock from the fire pit that represented the furnace of Orion.

'If this is the Furnace of Orion, that is the Fire of Nimrod, then when God asked Abraham to sacrifice his son in the fire then it was the same cosmic teaching. Then the background behind God in the Creation of Adam painting in the Vatican is the same cosmic wisdom'. – I was daydreaming.

"Mitakuye Oyasin." – I pushed the second stone inside the sweat lodge to my wife. She did the sage and the cedar blessings. Once she prayed over the rock that was still on the pitchfork, she carefully maneuvered the hot rock with two deer antlers into the pit off my fork. She rolled the rock to the side of the pit to make room for the next stone. We were symbolically handling the rock inside Mother Earth that was responsible for life on the globe. I participated in a few Bible studies, even with my Freemasonic buddies, but not once I felt the simplicity of the cosmic secrets presented to me with such clarity. Spirit was talking to me, generating thoughts of comparative mythology, and providing me with explanations to understand the hidden meanings in simple earthbound religious practices. Working with the hot volcanic rocks in the ceremony gave me a spiritual feeling.

We finished loading the stones inside the sweat lodge and before I climbed inside, I handed my wife the water bucket with a wooden ladle. My mind again was roaming as wild buffaloes roll on the big open prairie. I began to recall that my ancestors, the Sumerian Egyptian Magyars named the Mountain Goat 'Kanna–m' and showed a Can or a Vase. This Kanna-m was criminally mispronounced as 'Khnemu' by the Egyptologists. They did not care that both the Sumerians and the Hungarians called the CAN vase 'Kanna'.

This Egyptian creator god or even Hebrew Scape Goat - whose hieroglyphic sign was a 'Can' (=Kanna) vase, fused in my mind with the Hebrew water drawing ceremony at Rosh Hashanah. The first time that ceremony was performed by a rabbi in public in Israel was in the Hebrew Year of 5775 that is the year of 2015. That is 7 years before the 2021 / 2022. Did the Hebrew Year 5775 start the biblical 7 years of Bounty, before we would experience the 7 years of Famine?

I was understandably a little disappointed thinking how many millions of people from different religions and spiritualities were keeping these ceremonies alive, but practically none of them understood the cosmic wisdoms. Our religious leaders attached made up false information as to the origin of the ceremonies.

Most of the ceremonies could have been performed by animals from the 'Planet of the Apes' with the amount of understanding we humans possessed about these secrets. It seemed that for the majority people the ceremonies only meant to reach a closeness to God, to feel spiritual – but without the understanding why those ceremonies were designed in a certain way in the first place. I seen a need to write a book about the explanations of the origins of these ceremonies, but who has the time. We are already too late.

I climbed into the sweat lodge on all four squeezing by Eva, and I took a seat across my wife on the left side. She looked at me and nodded, which I knew meant to close the door. I reached out to pull down the door flap and the inside of the lodge became pitch black. Now we were symbolically sitting inside Mother Earth. She poured a spoonful of water on the volcanic rocks that began hissing with intense heat and the augmentation of unbearable humidity. The heat was so powerful that I had to place the towel in front of my face not to have it burnt. Jesus in the desert for 40 days came to my mind. 'I can do this'. The physical suffering is never as bad as the spiritual remorse.

"Whey haya heya heya heyo." - Eva began drumming and singing the first song of the first door. I picked up the rhythm and started singing with her. It was the blessing of the Four Direction song, starting with the direction of the West. Four songs we sang for each door. We took 5 – 10 minutes breaks in between the doors and the flap kept opened to lessen the heat and humidity.

"Close the door." – Eva asked. This was after the third healing round, and we had a lot of good prayers and discussions. After the third round we completed the healing round, and we were starting into the last door of the thanksgiving. A hard round for some including myself.

As we were sitting in the last round Eva poured the remaining water on the stones. The heat and humidity were so intense I was not sure I can stay in there. I began to see spirits, or I was just having a bad case of dehydration induced hallucination. The top of the lodge miraculously opened, and the sky was limitless. It was the afternoon still as we were completing the ceremony, but as I started going into spirit, the sky was now started looking like it was a pitched-black night. There were so many stars in the sky that the whole firmament appeared like it was constructed to fit a Hollywood movie screen. Falling stars appeared from all different directions and they organized into a spiral dance. In the middle of the twirling stars 24 elders appeared sitting in the sky. One of them separated out of the circle and took its place in the center. The elders were spiraling down toward the top of the lodge. They were in the sitting position without any chairs, underneath them. They were slowing their speed of rotation and the one in the center took the hoodie off his head. It was Jesus Christ, my Savior. I screamed.

"Jesus Christ, I have to confess to You. While I was in a coma on a ventilator, I had some strange and bad dreams." – I shared my concerns with the Lord. He placed His index finger in front of His mouth to tell me to quiet down. I realized that I was so loud it was disturbing.

"What happened Son?" – Christ asked innocently, while I was sure He knew everything about me. He was aware of all the thoughts I ever had, good or bad.

"I went to the prophet school, and You were one of my guides. I had to go through a gate. It was terrible. I never had a bad dream that was felt so real." – I admitted.

"What gate was it?" You need to tell me with your own words." – Jesus Christ insisted. I got nervous and I could not say a word. What if He does not even know about it and all my blabbering will only make me look bad in the eyes of the Lord.

"The gate … " – that was all I could say.

"I need to know more about that gate in intimate details. Talk to me Son." – Christ encouraged me.

"The narrow gate with the angry bees!" – Eva jumped into the conversation unexpectedly.

"What, you knew about it?" – I turned to my wife.

"We were there together honey." – Eva talked to me in an apologetic voice.

"Christ, I don't know what to say." – I admitted to the Lord.

"Don't say anything. Let me speak. … I am very proud of both of you." – Christ informed us.

The rest of the elders slowly circled around in the sky as if they sat on the merry-go-around of a peaceful tornado. There were some we recognized. Thoth, Horus, Moses, Abraham, Mohammed, Buddha, Red Cloud, John Smith, Vishnu, L. Ron Hubbard, Albert Pike, Mithra, Crazy Horse, the Chief of the African Dogon tribe, an Australian

Aborigine and a few others we could not recognize, or we did not remember the names. Behind them new rows of spiritual leaders appeared forming a concentric type of ripple in the sky. Every color and every culture that ever existed and praised the name of God was present in this funnel like hurricane. There had to be at least 144,000 spiritual leader swirling in the sky creating a reverberation that reported back to the Almighty God.

"I am proud of you two for keeping God as ONE. You were able to see that the same One God created everything in our Universe. Rather than fighting other religions you were able to see the messages wrapped in the same Astronomy and Cosmology that everybody used throughout the ages. You passed your first test. You are now allowed to take the test of prophets. It does not matter to know if the Red Cloud comes this Christmas or the next one. What matters is that you understand the process.

"We are all one!" - Christ signaled to the others and they all started spiraling toward the center. One by one they fused into the body of Christ and became one with him. It happened so fast, but everybody who was in the sky fused with the ones who were the closest and they all finally fused into Christ.

We don't remember how we completed the ceremony. When we looked up, we both were back in our dome house. We cleaned up and dressed.

"Do you want to go out and watch the stars?" – Eva asked me.

"Nothing else would make me happier." – I answered.

"Where are we going from here?" – my wife wondered.

"Wherever the Holy Spirit will take us." – was my answer.

"I like that." – Eva agreed and smiled at me. At this point we both felt that no matter what happens to us – we live forever on this side of the veil or on the other side where spirits dwell – but we do it truthfully. We understood that the Almighty God is pure Cosmic Truth. He is All of Nature, everything that has ever been thought of and was created exist because of Him. That is a miracle we will never fully understand. Our faith remained strong.

THE END
Of Part One